Six Hundred Daffodils

A Journey in Love and Spiritual Growth

❦ ❦

Chris Snyder

You are a special, unique person

Chris Snyder

KENDALL/HUNT PUBLISHING COMPANY
4050 Westmark Drive   Dubuque, Iowa 52002

Front cover photo courtesy of Jo Jeanne Callaway

Copyright © 1997 by Christopher Snyder

Library of Congress Catalog Card Number: 97-74032

ISBN 0-7872-4275-6

Printed in the United States of America

10 9 8 7 6 5 4 3 2 1

Dedication

This book is dedicated to my loving and passionate wife, my understanding mother, my son Taylor, and especially Jo Jeanne Callaway, without her true love, guidance and inspiration this book would not be possible.

I wandered lonely as a cloud
That floats on high o'er vales and hills,
When all at once I saw a crowd,
A host of golden daffodils;
Beside the lake, beneath the trees,
Fluttering and dancing in the breeze.

Wordsworth

Contents

Roadblocks to Spirituality

A Few More Thoughts . . .

Acknowledgments

My Personal Journal
May 9, 1997

"It is a wonderful, clear spring night with just a touch of red in the sky to the west where the sun is setting on another day and the completion of my book. The journey of self-discovery, love and deepening faith in God has been an absolute joy experienced in the writing of this book. But the journey will continue! Another book? I would think so.

There are a few people I would like to thank for their support, love and encouragement. I would first like to thank my loving wife for her patience on those long nights when I needed to write and rewrite. I would also like to thank Dr. Jo Jeanne Callaway, without her guidance, love and inspiration this endeavor would not have been possible. Finally, I would like to thank God. For without the Creator, we would not be here.

I would like to leave you with one last thought. During an interview, late in psychologist Carl Jung's life, he was asked if he believed in God. Jung said, **"I know there is a God."** I **know that too!**"

Chris Snyder

I am certain of nothing but the holiness of the Heart's affections and the truth of the Imagination.

John Keats

Introduction

To put it simply, this book is about my incredible spiritual journey in both discovering true love, my deep and true inner self, and God as my companion. If you don't believe in God, that is fine. I have learned to pass no judgment. Just as a beginning find a higher power to believe in. Examples of a higher power could be the love that flows through all of us, the energy of life, the exquisite beauty of the daily setting sun or the bright stars on a clear, tranquil night. Just find something you are comfortable with and believe in its power and energy.

Back to me for a moment, I have and still am having an extraordinary spiritual journey overflowing with love and extreme joy that I want to share directly with you. It may deeply heal you in ways that you can't believe imaginable. In the words of Robert Frost, *"Education hangs around until you catch on."* Or maybe this one suits you better, *"Education is not the filling of a pail, but the lighting of a fire."* And one has certainly been lit deep inside me.

And I want to share it . . . share the fire, the inspiration, the discovery, the true love, the deep understanding . . . I want to share it with you. Because when it comes right down to it that is all that matters . . . Sharing with and truly loving each other and God. If you can make it that simple everything will work out, and you will find your life fulfilled, and filled with joy and love . . . and you will feel complete . . . whole.

Chris Snyder

chapter one

Who We Are

> *"I'm just not myself,"*
> *baseball great Ty Cobb exclaims.*
> *A women's reply, "Who is?"*
> *from the HBO movie* **Cobb**

That simple, short quote is the very essence of what is wrong with most of us. We don't know, so we don't show, our true inner selves. We are like character actors in a movie, running around pretending to be what we are supposed to be in a certain situation . . . hiding our true selves. We build up tremendously high walls, fortresses to shelter and to protect our fragile egos. There is no reason to be open and vulnerable. We are too likely to get hurt, laughed at or taken advantage of for revealing our deep thoughts and feelings. The more we pretend, the more we begin to believe in all the different "masks" we create and wear. The ultimate truth is we are lying to ourselves. We slowly lose touch with our inner self, and then suddenly notice we are saying things like, *"I'm just not myself"* or *"I'm not sure how I feel or what exactly I am feeling."* Now, we are lost, frustrated, anxious and depressed. Those words begin to represent our out-of-touch feelings. Instead of saying, *"I am sad and lonely,"* we begin saying, *"I am depressed."*

At this point we continue in our day-to-day masquerade or, if we are touched by grace, we begin to search for the truth. I believe that search first has to begin with God. Not finding God, but believing in his existence. (I would like to apologize for referring to God in the traditionally masculine sense, but I have done so for simplicity rather than any firm belief in gender.) Now I know some of you are saying, God . . . I don't know about that. I am not going to try and convert you, but let me give you my proof of his existence.

My Personal Journal
November 10, 1996

"There is a God!! Such an unambiguous, succinct sentence, but what incredible strength, support, love, grace and faith it proclaims! I truly realized it today. There is a God! I am sure of that! Everything I have ever prayed for has been answered. I prayed for love, genuine love, and it was answered in my wife, Kris, my mother and father, and my son's birth. Let me backtrack a moment and define genuine love and marriage by two perfect quotes. Scott Peck writes in **The Road Less Traveled**: 'Genuine love not only respects the individuality of the other but actually seeks to cultivate it, even at the risk of separation or loss. I define love thus: The will to extend one's self for the purpose of nurturing one's own or another's spiritual growth.' In reference to marriage, the prophet Kahil Gibran speaks to us:

> 'But let there be spaces in your togetherness,
> and let the winds of heaven dance between you
>
> Love one another, but make not a bond of love:
> Let it rather be a moving sea between the shores of your souls.
>
> Fill each other's cup but drink not from one cup.
> Give one another of your bread but eat not from the same loaf

Sing and dance and be joyous, but let each one of you be alone,
Even as the strings of a lute are alone though they quiver
with the same music.

Give your hearts, but not into each other's keeping.
For only the hand of Life can contain your hearts.
And stand together yet not too near together:
For the pillars of the temple stand apart, and the
oak tree and the cypress grow not in each other's shadow.'

Love was also answered by my in-laws Ted and Mary . . . it
was answered in my very soul. It is answered in the shining
sun, the soothing wind . . . it is answered in the brilliant stars
and the heavenly light of the moon. It, love, is all around me, I
just had to open my eyes a little to see it.

Today is a revelation.

Today is incredible joy.

Today is now . . . I now know there is a God.

I prayed over and over for patience . . . it was answered by five
days without electricity . . . it was answered by a wrecked car
(no one was hurt), and then a wrecked rental car . . . it was
answered by waiting for a long time to see what would happen
at my job. Once again all I had to do was open my eyes to see
it.

I prayed for vulnerability and for God to break down my inner
walls . . . the prayer was answered . . . I feel pain in other's
suffering. I feel happiness and love in others' joyous moments. I
feel . . . I feel deep inside me. I feel so much now sometimes it
is overwhelming, but it is wonderful . . . it is glorious! I know
who I am. I am loving . . . I am whole . . . I feel complete.

There are so many pieces of life's giant puzzle I can see and
grasp now, and the extraordinary thing about it is the puzzle is
even bigger and more beautiful.

I am filled with so much emotion now . . . I used to feel nothing. It is energizing! It is fantastic!

I want more!! I want to share it with others. There is so much to life we are missing. I don't want to miss anything. I don't want to hide anymore. I am going to be myself, my true inner self. I feel complete joy!! Thanks be to God!"

I wanted to share that journal entry early with you in this book. It has taken me a long time to reach that point, but spiritual journeys are meant to last a lifetime. I will devote a whole chapter in this book to journal writing and the incredible insights and revelations that can come from doing it. Don't worry, it is not hard to do . . . it is much easier than you think.

Back to the journal entry, if you find yourself having trouble with God's existence, at least try and take that first step and believe in a higher power than you. Then you can believe in yourself. I may sound like I have it reversed . . . you should believe in yourself before God. No. Wrong. God is a very deep part of you. He is your subconscious. When you believe in Him or a higher power, you are believing in a deep part of you. Then you will come to love yourself, and that leads you to truly love others because self-love and love of others go hand in hand.

chapter two

Who We Should Be . . .

We should be loving, caring, trusting, deep-thinking, compassionate individuals who are in touch with our true inner selves. Our true inner selves are filled with innocent, pure love and the strong light of God. There is a confident power within this light. *"God is gold and there is a nugget of gold in each one of us."* But we first must find that nugget. We need direction. We need a path. A path of self-discovery that leads to faith, forgiveness, and ultimately to God.

The purpose of this book is relatively simple, but the work is conscious and hard. And the results are joyous and peaceful. The purpose is to help you find your direction. With a few simple ideas that are not new but have been overlooked.

There is what I call life within life. There is a whole life within us that most of us choose to ignore. We are far too concerned with making a fast buck or becoming *one up* on our materialistic friends. The media and television have taught us that major problems can be worked out with money or during a thirty-minute sitcom with two commercial breaks.

Let me ask you a question. Have you ever felt psychological pain or do you choose *not to go there?* In other words, do you avoid the pain associated with life? With growth? Are you aware of the overwhelming feeling and deep healing power of true love? Or are you like most who are numb to what love really is? I know the feeling. As I will write again later, I prayed to God for years to let me feel love because I couldn't. But finally my prayers were answered. That is why I am writing this book. And I now realize with feeling love, comes pain. I was blind to love and all other emotions. Now I can **feel.** I can feel every emotion and, whether it is bad or good emotion, it is wonderful to feel.

We all avoid pain. It is only natural. But we must face the pain of life in order to feel love. To feel the presence of God. There have been many times when I have broken down and cried because of happiness or sadness, just because of feeling those deep feelings that swell up inside me. I just want to feel, because it is our human feelings and ability to reason that separates us from the animals of this beautiful planet. I feel connected to life, and grateful for my existence whether it be bad or good. Just to **feel,** and not to block those feelings is a truly magnificent experience. But to feel we must be able to think deeply, and, unfortunately, most would rather live life simplistically. Thinking on only a shallow level. What matters to those people is whatever will get us *to the top,* at all costs, squashing anyone who gets in our way. We are selfish when we need to be selfless. To be selfish, though, is what we are taught from the very beginning, and are constantly bombarded with throughout our short lives. The pressures are enormous, and our fragile egos usually fall to them. You must be thin, beautiful, dressed impeccably, and drink the right beer *to fit in.* It is ironic that most people who are remembered for some achievement didn't *fit in.* You **can be yourself,** because each one of us is truly unique and special. But *being yourself* is tough because others close to you will see you as slightly different. Someone who rocks the boat and doesn't follow the societal norm.

Life is full of struggles, but it is how we handle those struggles that defines us as a person. We grow from meeting daily hardships head-on and delaying gratification. I believe we must face those struggles on a spiritual basis. Spirituality is the great missing piece in life and psychotherapy today. Now, do not shy away. Spirituality does not mean you have to be a believer in God. I have met a number of atheists and agnostics who are spiritual in nature. Their belief lies in a higher power. They believe in love, nature or a special relationship that develops between two close friends. The ultimate goal, though, is to come to know there is a God.

The following chapters are designed to show you how to get to know your true self. The inner self that hides behind the facade you let the world see. The facade you present shows you have it all together . . . whoever has the most toys when he dies wins. Right? There are also chapters and spiritual exercises to help you let go of the pain, resentment and anger we hold onto from the past, and feel and understand your emotions during the present. And that is exactly how you should live, in the present. Not the past or future, but the moment of now.

One way of doing this is keeping a daily journal. A spiritual journey's journal if you like. Because, if you choose to read further, that is what I hope you are truly beginning. A new and revealing journey in life and love. A journey to new heights and deep insights. And I can tell you from personal experience this journey will change the way you see life. If you would have told me that I would be writing this two years ago, I would have laughed in your face. Now I have to write this because it is too special to keep secret.

*   *   *   *   *

I gave no name to this section of the "Who We Should Be" chapter, because I wanted you to read it with no preconceived ideas of what it is going to be about. I wanted your mind, spirit and soul completely open to all possibilities.

Do you believe in God?

If your answer is "yes," I have another question for you.

Do you *know* there is a God?

I ask this because there is a substantial difference in believing and knowing. That difference is certainty. When you read the question,

"Do you know there is a God?" Did you hesitate for just a moment? If you did, that is still just a belief.

To say we believe in something, some cause or someone, means we possess a little doubt. We are leaning in that direction, but we need more information to make up our mind completely.

To know something or know someone, like God, we are wholly certain of its validity, or in this case, God's existence. I fear many people are stuck somewhere in the middle. Between belief in God, and *knowing* there is a God.

That is the main purpose of this book. To help you to *know* there is a God.

Earlier in this book, I wrote that you don't have to be a believer in God. Just find a higher power, like love, to believe in. That is the starting point. Just a belief in something higher than yourself. Along the journey your belief will slowly turn to a convinced knowledge of a higher power. Then to a belief in God, and hopefully you will finally exclaim, "I know there is a God."

By no means is this process quick. It took me thirty years to come to this realization. And by no means does the journey end there. Actually, I feel with every new day, the journey is starting all over again. That is why I write in a daily journal.

chapter three

Your Journey's Journal

I suffer from panic attacks. I can remember my first one like it was yesterday. Even though it happened over ten years ago. I was spending summer break from college in Hilton Head, South Carolina. Working late hours at a local bar and living with a group of guys from my fraternity house in a small two bedroom apartment. It was supposed to be a fun summer; a little work and lots of play. But actually it turned out to be the turning point in my life. I awoke one night at about two in the morning. My heart was pounding, my body soaked in sweat, and my throat felt like it was going to close up. A tremendous fear swept over me. I thought I was going to die! I was sure of it! Then my head went numb, and I actually felt like I was on the edge of being possessed and taken over by some evil unknown force. My heart raced, and I began to lose my breath, almost to the point of hyperventilating. I kept wondering, what is going on? Why is this happening? Am I going completely nuts? That may be the worst part of the attacks. The terrible, sinking feeling you are going crazy, and at any moment you could lose total control. Lucky people who have never suffered from a panic attack should be thankful. They are extremely cruel and excruciating experiences.

Eventually, I calmed down some, but from that point onward extreme anxiety and panic attacks became a routine part of my daily life. For awhile I turned to alcohol for self-medication. Luckily though, I quit. (But that subject is for another chapter.) For years my schoolwork suffered; my family life suffered; my whole life suffered. Then, by the grace of God, about six years ago a doctor recognized my condition, and put me on some medication that really helped. I took Buspar daily for a little over two years, and then slowly weaned myself off of it. I thought I was cured! The anxiety and panic attacks were gone. They lay quiet for about three years, and then returned with an incredible vengeance in May 1996. I was going through a tremendous life decision that probably triggered their ugly return. This time, though, I decided to face the problem, with a little help from my mother, head-on. Mom introduced me to a psychiatrist who would change my life. Her name is Dr. Jo Jeanne Callaway. I consider her now a soulmate. We have a special, deep bond that is hard to put into words other than love. In a short time she helped me to recognize my deep, but hidden, spirituality. She helped me get in touch with my inner self. She helped me discover love and feel genuine true love. All of these things were already part of me but I didn't realize it because I had built up such huge walls to protect myself. Jo Jeanne helped me discover myself by introducing me to the art of journal writing. My spiritual journey had begun. I believe, now, so much in the deep healing power of keeping a journal, a diary if you will. I now thank God for the panic attacks because, without them, I would never have found out who and what I truly am.

When I was first told to try and keep a journal, I thought I could never do this. What would I possibly write about? Jo Jeanne said, *"Whatever comes to your mind. Write about the day's events. Write about your observations of life. Pick a chapter in a book you are reading and write down your thoughts about that."* Here is my first journal entry from June of 1996:

My Personal Journal
June 3, 1996

"I do feel like I am starting a long journey. I'm not sure at all where it will take me, but it is something deep within me I must do. It's hard to sit here and think of a topic to write about. I have this feeling, though, once I get the hang of it, the words will start flowing. I decided I would attempt to find a subject to write about by thumbing through Scott Peck's book **The Road Less Traveled**. I came to page fifty and found the sentence I highlighted 'Truth or reality is avoided when it's painful. We can revise our maps (I would call maps: old ways of thinking) when we have the discipline to overcome the pain. To have such discipline, we must be totally dedicated to the truth.' The truth is something I need to work on, and work on a lot. I have always found it easier to lie than suffer the consequences of the truth. To this day when people ask me why I don't drink, I usually (always) tell them I am allergic to alcohol. Which is partly true. My liver doesn't metabolize alcohol correctly, but the real reason I don't drink is because I am an alcoholic. I admit I am powerless over alcohol. In college it was easier to drink and avoid the struggles of school. Starting today, I am going to make a conscious effort to just tell people the truth if they ask me why I don't drink. I have nothing to be ashamed of. It has been ten years since I last took a drink. I believe that is quite an accomplishment. I must be honest, though, I have had a couple of non-alcoholic beers over the years. It makes me feel like I cheated a little. But honestly, I have no urge to drink anymore . . . it has crossed my mind a few times, but I know deep inside that it wouldn't solve my problems or help out in any way.

But back now to truth and honesty. When I do pray (I need to work on praying more) I always pray to God to help me become a more honest person. In the past year or so, I do believe, I have become more honest. But I do regret situations in the past where I wish I had not lied. One instance comes to mind. Several years ago in college I had a friend in my fraternity who had a girlfriend I also knew. Trying to be cool or superior to my friend, I lied to him and told him I had slept with his girlfriend. Well, to make a long story short, she confronted me with this lie, and I lost two friends very quickly, and who knows how many other people were told about the incident who then lost trust in me."

Six months later I have filled about five journals with life experiences, memories, and prayers to God. My anxiety has subsided, and I feel in touch deeply with my inner self and God.

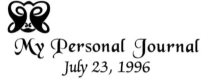

My Personal Journal
July 23, 1996

"It's a beautiful night . . . cool, no breeze, half a slightly vanilla-colored moon peeking through the quiet trees over my shoulder. It is so ironic how I have discovered my love for the outdoors at night since I had my first panic attack ever in the middle of the night.

I have wanted to write about this now for a couple of nights so I am kind of excited. I am not sure exactly what to call it, so I figure the Grace of God is the best thing for now.

What I am talking about is this new part of me I have discovered from journal writing deep, deep within. It's hard to describe, but I will try and do my best.

There seems to be this small part, deep in the left side of my brain, that I have either uncovered or am in the process of discovering. Strength, stability, knowing what to do emanates from this blessed area. I seem to not worry at all when decisions come from this Grace-touched place. Actually, I seem to worry less about the things I have the least control over. I still push myself to the limit to get too much accomplished, but there is a new part of me that is so powerful, strong and confident.

It is like a patch of fresh green grass in a newly found land that I thought didn't exist. I'm not saying it's the end to all my problems, but it's an undiluted thing when it pops up and knows the correct answer without a doubt, without reservation. However I discovered this special place within, I pray to you, Lord it stays with me and continues to grow. It is a strong feeling and presence, and lately it seems to be there when I need it most."

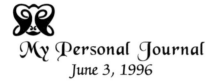

My Personal Journal
June 3, 1996

"A few minutes ago (midnight Friday night) I was sitting on the porch "imaging" that special place inside me I have found, and I thought I would try and put it into words.

Imagine an absolutely picture perfect night . . . full of summer stars. I am out on a quiet beach. The air is cool . . . the breeze refreshing. All is totally calm. As I look out over the ocean the moon, a full one, is just gently rising out over the water. The soft light rippling gently off the almost placid ocean. Ripple after ripple . . . like waves of energy. From the light of the moon, not too far from shore, I can see a small boat. I can see the outline of one person in that boat . . . the moon is His spotlight. He beckons to me to come to the end of a long wooden dock. As I walk down the dock, step by step, I grow calmer, stronger and a deep sense of love settles over my body and soul. As I approach the end of the dock the man in the boat has docked, and is waiting for me. I arrive and am overwhelmed with love, support and a bright light. I realize at once this is God in the boat. He asks me to join Him. In awe, in wonder, and in peace I sit down in the boat, and God paddles away as the full moon rises out of the water.

God does not look like I imagined . . .

He looks like me . . .

For I was created in His image . . .

As we pull away from the dock, I look back over my shoulder and the view has changed. No longer is there a beach, but many other things. To the left is a bustling city . . . at the center the deep sand dunes of a desert, and to the right tall snow-topped mountains rising from the rolling hills of a deep summer-green countryside.

'Where are we going?' I ask.

The Lord replies, 'Your life is in my hands, I will steer and guide you. Trust in me. Enjoy the journey, but learn. There will be some suffering . . . some difficult times, but I will be there, and you will make it. Always remember that special place in your soul . . . come to me there when you need me.'

'I will', I said.

Glory be to God. Thanks for the Grace you have touched me with."

Journal writing is your own personal form of therapy. It is just you and your thoughts. No inhibitions because you don't have to let anyone read it. But eventually you will because you will want to share your revelations and deep understanding with others. Just as I am doing.

It amazes me some nights when I think I am going to write just a little and seven pages come pouring out. It is mind clearing . . .

tranquilizing. And over time, as you see your thoughts on paper, you begin to notice patterns. Patterns in your life you can change for the better.

Without journal writing I would not be where I am today. A total belief in God, in deep contact with my inner self, and at peace with myself and the world around me.

Try writing tonight. Pick up a piece of paper, and just pick out any subject that comes to mind. You will be amazed just how your thoughts turn into words on paper. After a few nights of writing you will also begin to see how nature plays a deep role in your emerging spiritual life.

Your First Journal Entry

If you have never kept a journal before, let's give it a trial run. Throughout the first day you decide to keep a journal try to be cognizant of and extremely focused on what is happening all around you. At the end of the day, write down any observations or feelings you may have had. Try to be specific and determine what *triggered* any emotional response.

*Date:*_____

_____

_____

_____

_____

_____

_____

_____

_____

_____

_____

_____

_____

_____

_____

_____

_____

_____

_____

_____

_____

_____

_____

_____

Journal Entry
Day Two

On this day try and look for things that go your way. You may call them just coincidences, but I like to say it is God's grace.

*Date:*_____

_____

_____

_____

_____

_____

_____

_____

_____

_____

_____

_____

_____

_____

_____

_____

_____

_____

_____

_____

_____

_____

_____

_____

Journal Entry
Day Three

If you can find the time, and the weather is cooperating, take the time to enjoy nature for just a few moments. Write about how it makes you feel and the beauty of the earth around you.

Date:_____

_____

_____

_____

_____

_____

_____

_____

_____

_____

_____

_____

_____

_____

_____

_____

_____

_____

_____

_____

_____

_____

_____

_____

chapter four

Nature's Gift

When you are walking alone,
lift up your spirit and listen to the sermon preached
to you by the trees, the shrubs, the sky and the whole world.
Notice how they preach to you a sermon full of Love,
of praise of God, and how they invite you to glorify the sublimity
of that sovereign Artist who has given them being.

Saint Paul of the Cross

I have written many times in my journals about nature and the incredible effects it can have upon you and your soul. This revealing quote could not sum it up better.

Just take a few moments on a glorious day, take a walk and listen to the wind in the trees and the symphony they create. At that point you will be living in the present. Living moment by moment . . . second by second. It is truly a remarkable gift to you from God. It is Grace. It is a mind-clearing gift . . . at that point nothing else matters.

As I write this on an airplane at 35,000 feet, I can see nature's (God's) beauty. God's masterpiece in the sky above and below. The clouds float delicately above pastures of lush green and hues of golden yellow and bright red. This breathtaking scenery glorifies the Artist that has painted it.

My Personal Journal
October 1, 1996

"What an incredible day! The sun is bright and warm, and I am relaxing in a hammock. The sun is flickering through the wind-blown trees like a candle dancing in the wind. The wind . . . the sound of the wind is nature's ballet. It is one of the most incredible, refreshing sounds there is. The artistic beauty of manmade music can be stunning, but it doesn't hold a chord with the beauty of the wind. It is a symphony . . . it quiets, then grows stronger in a perfect rhythm. Every whisper of wind clears my mind of all thoughts, and I am truly living in the present. The present . . . what peace and joy it brings with no strings attached. I may not be able to be perfect, but nature knows how.

Just listen to the wind and let the sun dance on your face . . . what a precious moment.

I am learning quickly the effect nature can have . . . no future, no past, right now, right here. There is something very special about this place earth.

I have found a special place in my soul, now I have found a magical setting outside my inner self that has a direct connection to my inner self. Thank you, Lord . . . this is truly magnificent.

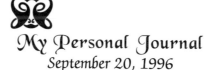

My Personal Journal
September 1, 1996

"The sounds of a late summer night are truly captivating. The crickets, the locusts, and the rest of God's earthly creatures creating a musical masterpiece all their own. Never quite the same pattern. Just an intertwined ensemble of individual melodies.

In a certain way like life. Sometimes the patterns can be similar, but most of life's events are intertwined and affected by others whether it be directly or indirectly.

I believe if you are in touch with your soul, with your heart, and with God . . . your song . . . your symphony can be truly beautiful. Trust and love yourself . . . trust and love God . . . let Him direct and compose the symphony of your life.

The music will be from your heart and beautiful."

My Personal Journal
September 20, 1996

"It is seven o'clock and the sun is setting on yet another day. I am lying in bed facing two windows hung with venetian blinds, and the golden yellow glow from the setting sun is filtering through, lighting the room in a magical soft light. Something similar to shards of brilliant thought and understanding filtering through your subconscious to conscious mind when you least expect it.

Finding a beautiful sunset is like stumbling upon a small piece of our lives' ever growing puzzle.

There is so much more to real life, real living, than work, paying bills and being stuck in long lines of traffic.

There is a child's brilliant smile, an unexpected soul connection between two people, and, of course, beautiful sunsets.

I strongly believe I happen upon this one by God's grace to remind me there is a good side to a bad day or life situation, and if you wait long enough, have patience, a magnificent sunrise will follow . . . filling your mind, your heart, your very soul with new thoughts and inspirations for the start of a new day . . . a new beginning.

My sunrise, my spiritual journey, began a few months ago, and I am still basking in its mellow guiding light and ultimate glory."

My Personal Journal
September 17, 1996

"As the light of day gives way to the darkness of night, and the stars fill the sky like diamonds on black velvet, the rhythm of the night slows and so should I.

Not all can be accomplished in one day, even though I believe it can . . . one day, one minute, one second at a time. Things that can be put off should be . . . relax and enjoy every moment with nature."

Before I started my spiritual journey I was not in touch with nature, like a number of other items. I now believe you can not fully be on a spiritual journey without truly opening your eyes and allowing God's created nature to do its magical, breathless work.

Nature can have a truly profound, deep-meaning effect on you in many ways. Let me tell you the story behind the title of this book . . . *Seven Hundred Daffodils.*

Jo Jeanne once told me a story about her departed husband. The time was late fall, and she was in the painstaking process of planting some daffodils around their house so next spring they would emerge from their sleep and show their simple beauty. She asked her son Christopher for a little help digging the holes as the ground was growing hard because of the upcoming winter. Her husband Lee said, *"I'll dig the holes if you let me plant the damn things where I want!"* Never having planted flowers before he stuck all twenty-five in one group together in the front yard.

Next spring arrived and the daffodils bloomed in their special glory, and Lee was stunned by their absolute beauty. He thought he had created a masterpiece.

Spring and summer came and went, and it was time to plant daffodils again for the coming season. On his way back from a trip, Lee stopped at a discount flower shop somewhere in Oklahoma and bought seven hundred bulbs! That's right . . . Seven Hundred!!

Lee preceded to plant all seven hundred in their large front yard . . .

What a tremendous surprise next spring . . .

Seven hundred daffodils dancing in the wind in a sprightly dance . . . The power and beauty of nature is breathtaking. Every spring Jo Jeanne is surrounded by the memory of her late husband, by seven hundred golden flowers.

Those daffodils represent the spirit and love that still remains after his death. But in order to fully feel love you must learn to *let go* of the negative emotions that you carry around from years of confrontations and *beating* yourself up for failures. Only when you can *let go* will there be a place in your heart for growing love.

chapter five

Letting Go and Forgiveness

I realize the words *letting go* can be quite alarming. Questions may quickly *pop* into your mind, *"What am I suppose to let go of, and how will this possibly help me?"* Do not be fearful, though, of *letting go*. Through spiritual release nothing will be lost . . . only good will be gained. *Letting go* is a form of forgiveness, and will truly help you to heal in many ways. By *letting go* of old painful emotions of anger, frustration, rejection, disappointment and resentment you are setting your spirit free. You are allowing the space filled by those old emotions and memories to become open and receptive once again. And by opening parts of your spirit, your true inner self, you are permitting new ideas, new positive thoughts and love to quickly fill that recently acquired *space* inside you. In other words *let go* of what you do not want to make room for what you truly crave. That is love, compassion, being, and a closer relationship with others and God.

Anger is a powerful emotion you really need to let go of . . . if you don't, it will slowly consume your life and take up more needed space in your heart. This can happen even after many years have passed since the anger causing incident. Since you can not change people who have angered and hurt you, *let go* of the pain, and you will find an inner peace and serenity immediately occurs. You are basically healing old wounds. Even if you believe you are still correct in your disagreement, *let go* of the anger and resentment. Try saying this to yourself about an incident in which you have been wronged: *"I fully and freely forgive you. I let you go as far as I am concerned. That incident between us is over and finished forever. I do not wish to hurt you anymore. I freely wish you no harm. I am free and so are you, and all is well again between us."*

Through *letting go* your power of attracting good is increased dramatically.

 *A Spiritual Exercise*

Forgiveness

Sit for fifteen to twenty minutes each day and mentally or verbally forgive everyone you have had an argument or falling out with at sometime. Likewise, if you are upset with yourself for failures or mistakes, forgive yourself and set your spirit free. Those arguments or failures have happened in the past and can not be changed. So why dwell on them, and take up unnecessary space in your heart. Space that can be filled with much more, like love.

Now, you might be asking yourself what about the other person or persons involved in this dispute? I have forgiven them, but what good will that do? First, as I mentioned before, it will open more space in your heart and soul for new spiritual growth. Second, it will start the wheels of forgiveness in action and all involved will respond, be blessed, and the solution will appear.

You will be surprised, if you start this healing process, how many other repressed memories and hurtful emotions will begin floating back into your consciousness. Once this occurs, you can start *letting go* and forgiving these old emotions, clearing even more space to allow new love into your heart.

chapter six

Love

Earlier in this book I said I agree with Scott Peck's definition of love, *"as the will to extend one's self for the purpose of nurturing one's own or another's spiritual growth"* (Peck, Scott. *The Road Less Traveled*).

That definition is somewhat inadequate, though. Actually, any definition of love I have read or try to express in my own words doesn't encompass the entire true meaning of love. Love is far too vast, too large, and runs too deep, to be truly measured by mere words or sentences.

To each person love has its own special meaning, but it has to be an *effortfull,* "reaching out" love to be true.

Let me try to explain. I believe there are three types of love. The first is actually not love at all, but most of you will think I'm crazy for saying this. I am making reference to "love at first sight." This is an effortless type of love. As many people say, "I think I may be falling in love." That is effortless, and it is also a misconception about love. Even though your internal feelings, and external reactions are powerful and very passionate. You may believe that you deeply love either him or her, but in essence that is not true for a couple of reasons.

The experience of falling in love is very temporary. That is not to say that we will stop loving the person, but it is to say the feeling of burning excitement and lovingness that accompanies the experience of falling in love always passes. I am sure you have heard the statement, *"The honeymoon is over."* Scott Peck writes, *"But most of us feel our loneliness to be painful and yearn to escape from behind the walls of our individual identities to a condition in which we can be more unified with the world outside of ourselves. The experience of falling in love allows us this escape—temporarily. The essence of the phenomenon of falling in love is a sudden collapse of a section of an individual's ego boundaries, permitting one to merge his or her identity with that of another person. The sudden release of oneself, the explosive pouring out of oneself into the beloved, and the dramatic surcease of loneliness accompanying this collapse of ego boundaries, is experienced by most of us as ecstatic. We and our beloved are one! Loneliness is no more"* (Peck, Scott. *The Road Less Traveled*).

The definition of ego boundaries is similar to the walls, the fortresses we build up to protect our inner selves.

Another reason falling in love or love at first sight is not true love is because it is a sexually based attraction to another person. We fall in love when we are consciously or unconsciously sexually motivated.

Another misconception about love is dependent love. It may appear to be true, genuine love because it is a feeling that causes individuals to overly attach themselves to one another.

In college I worked for a suicide/crisis center named Headquarters. After a significant amount of training, I began *answering* the phones for eight hours at a time. Listening to people, and I mean intently listening to people, talk about their specific problems, and hopefully I would be able to guide them to a decision on what to do next, depending on what our conversation dictated. Listening is an important skill. It takes quite a lot of effort and energy to effectively listen.

I remember one call in which the person was threatening to commit suicide because his girlfriend had left him for another man. He said, *"I can't live without her. I love her so much."* Carefully, I told him, "I feel your pain, but what you feel is not true love." He became very angry, and I thought I had definitely said the wrong thing. For a moment he was quiet so I continued by saying, *"When you require another person for your survival, there is no choice or freedom in your relationship. When two people truly love each other they are certainly capable of living without each other, but they choose to live with each other."*

For a brief moment there was silence, and then he started to cry. *"Why can't she love me,"* he said. *"I felt so secure with her."* Again I had to remember this person threatened suicide when he had first called, so I had to thoughtfully choose my next words. I said, *"When you said "secure," what did you mean?"*

He answered, *I feel happy . . . I feel my life is complete, I don't feel, ahhh . . ."* I said, *Lonely?"* He said, "Yeah, lonely."

Lonely was a key word, and a tip-off that he was suffering from a dependent form of love. Our conversation continued for nearly seven hours. By the end I had done about six hours of listening and maybe one hour of talking. He finally said, *"I never would have committed suicide, but now I feel so insecure and alone."* He was a student at Kansas University and I suggested he seek counseling at the University hospital. The fees were very inexpensive if you were a student. He said, *"I will do that and thank you for listening. Can I call back anytime?"* "Anytime," I replied. I heard from him about five months later. All he called to say was thank you and that he had entered a new relationship with another woman. I said, *"Great,"* and he hung up.

Real, honest-to-goodness love is a self-enlarging experience. Its goal is spiritual growth for oneself and the beloved.

"When one has successfully extended one's limits, one has grown into a larger state of being. Thus the act of loving is an act of self-evolution even when the purpose of the act is someone else's

growth. It is through reaching toward evolution that we evolve" (Peck, Scott. *The Road Less Traveled*).

My Personal Journal
July 12, 1996

"Love is all that matters. It's what separates us . . . it's what brings us together . . . its results are beautiful . . . the creation of children . . . the bond that can't be broken . . . the ultimate self-sacrifice. For to truly love you must love yourself and be able to let go . . . let go and take the risk of naked vulnerability.

But it's worth it, and a loving bond between two people can't be broken, it can only grow. And if love is there, God is there, and that triangle is a force so strong that it is not measurable, and totally impenetrable. To live life to the fullest, I am realizing, you must let all your love go as much as you can."

I have this feeling I have cheated you slightly on the true meaning of love. It is not just a simple definition or a mere process of "letting go." And you are correct, there is much more to love. You must go deep inside yourself where true, innocent love still exists in its pure form. That is within your spirit.

Earlier I spoke of "falling in love" as being as temporary as warm weather is in the middle of January. It is a brief opening to your spirit, the true self that lives in all of us. Unfortunately, that opening closes quickly when the word *commitment* comes into being. In a relationship there are many psychological reasons why people do not commit. The main reason is when love is blocked by ego. Your ego and spirit are opposites to one another. Your ego wants material possessions, money, a high-paying job, security at any cost, and the ability to be right when others are perceived to be wrong. Have you ever been in a situation in which you feel the urge to fight for one side of an argument even when you believe that viewpoint to be incorrect? That is your ego expressing itself.

Your ego is a fortress hardened by years of constant battle with others. It wants to win at all costs. Your ego has built high walls to protect you from being taken advantage of by others. The ego's goals of pursuing material possessions, security and easily predictable outcomes, shuts out another person (your lover) unless he or she falls in line with your ego's personal agenda, or he or she comes to realize by your ego's influence that "I" am the important, controlling person in this relationship.

Spirit, on the other hand, is not concerned with what drives the ego. Your spirit wants being, true, pure love, freedom and creative opportunities. This is an entirely different level of desire, and when you reach it you can truly share your true self with another person without any detrimental conflict.

So, as you can see, your ego and spirit are opposites even though they co-habitate together inside your psyche. So how do you break through your ego boundaries and let your spirit run free? The core of such intimacy and sharing is surrender. It may sound simple, but your ego, at all costs, is not going to let it happen.

> *"Spiritually, no action is more important than surrender. Surrender is the tenderest impulse of the heart, acting out of love to give whatever the beloved wants. Surrender is being alert to exactly what is happening now, not imposing expectations from the past. Surrender is faith that the power of love can accomplish anything, even when you can not foresee the outcome of a situation"* (Chopra, Deepak. *The Path to Love*).

Now it may sound like surrender is hard work, and if it does, your ego is talking. But in reality it is not hard work it is *conscious* work.

Why should you surrender to another and allow yourself to be vulnerable? Because when you are spiritually committed in love, the husband/boyfriend sees God in his lover and the same is true for the other. He or she sees God in that person. Remember, God is Love, and Love is God, and God resides in each one of us. In our subconscious . . . in our spirit . . . in our true self.

A Child's Love

Taking an interest in the soul is a way of loving it. The ultimate cure comes from love, not from logic. Understanding doesn't take us very far in this work, but love, expressed in patient and careful attention, draws the soul in from its dispersion in problems and fascinations. It has been noted that most, if not all, problems brought to therapists are issues of that love. It makes sense then that the cure is also love.

Thomas Moore, *Care of the Soul*

A young child's love is innocent, pure and unconditional. You can see and feel its overpowering presence. It doesn't have a tremendous, strong ego blocking its precious flow. It flows freely, uninhibited. That form of love is what we should strive to get back in touch within our lives. A steadfastly flowing, unsullied love full of your true self with no need for response.

Unfortunately, many people have "strings" attached to their perceived love. "I love you, but will you do this for me? I have done so much for you. Can't you see that I love you?" There is helpful action involved, but that is not love in its true sense. It is a ploy of sidestepping love, sidestepping so your heart will not have to feel vulnerable, and open to rejection. Your ego protects you from harm. The only way to give true love is straight from the heart, wholly, with no "strings" attached. You *should not expect* something in return for the love you give. If you do, that is your ego talking.

True, pure love comes from the deep, inner self, your soul, and your soul does not need or want *excess baggage*-laden love. Still living deep within your soul is your original God-touched child's love. Innocent, pure and unconditional with no "strings" attached. It is possible to reach that love once again by surrender and risking naked vulnerability every waking moment of your life. When you feel love, fully express it, do not hold it back. If you hold it back that is a loss, and our ego feels that loss as very painful and destructive. This *loss* just reinforces your ego's beliefs that it is not worth risking being open and vulnerable. The ego feels it is better to be protected from any harm.

By pushing away and holding your true love inside, you will begin to slowly lose touch with it and, in return, feel empty, and even more uncomfortable trying to give it out.

Love can be a wonderful circle. When you give it freely it will return to you freely, without "strings" attached, in heart-filling ways.

*   *   *   *   *

When you ignore or deny love's existence, you are denying a special, positive part of you. Usually, we deny only the bad aspects of our self.

Denial of our defects in personality keeps us from becoming *whole*. We need to bring to the surface those deficient aspects of ourselves, and face what we feel is undesirable so we can become a *whole* person. We are not perfect, and by facing our faults we then can become able to work on them to make us a better, whole person. Personality traits we deny include: dishonesty, disrespect for our self and others, wrongly directed anger, irresponsibility, laziness, noncommitment, uncaring attitudes, "know-it-all" behavior, and the list goes on.

You can find out what faults you have by picking your boss or someone you have had conflict with and making a short list of the things you dislike strongly about the person. Those *dislikes* are often mirrored in ourselves. That person represents the faults we hide in our true selves. When those faults are realized in your conscious mind, you then can begin the process of change. Changing for the better. Changing to become a *whole* person.

My Personal Journal
February 17, 1996

"I felt the ultimate joy of love today. I was having a wonderful conversation with Jo Jeanne on the ultimate power of love. My ego boundaries dropped, and true love came flooding through. In that love was God. His presence was easily felt. The air in the room in which we sat became suddenly thick with an intense, loving energy. An energy of pure, innocent love. An intensity that is hard to fully explain. Love could be felt by both of us. A binding force that could not be broken. I was one with my spirit, and I was one with God. The experience was simply tremendous. It was the simplest grace of our Lord. If you have any doubts of God's existence, they would have been wiped away if you had been in that room. But this can happen to you. By conscious effort to surrender yourself to another person. Forget your ego-driven world, and choose to live a true, passionate life."

For years I thought I would never feel real love. I felt it was being blocked by some unmovable force. I prayed to God to let me feel and express my love. I almost got to the point where I believed I just wasn't going to feel or even recognize love. But, through prayer, love found me. And it started when I began loving myself because God enlightened me through prayer.

chapter seven

Prayer

For where the journey takes me does not matter
As long as I have a light to follow, the path is true
When the light is dim, prayer is the answer . . .
When the light is brilliant, prayer is thankfulness

Chris Snyder

One can not be on a true spiritual journey without prayer. Private prayer between you and God or your higher power. How can you know God or your true inner self unless you spend time alone with Him where He will speak to you in your mind and heart. As you know, God speaks to me from his waiting boat, docked at a pier on the ocean. You will discover your true self, insights, secrets, and answers of which you have never dreamed. It is hard to love someone, though, that you don't really know. Through private prayer you will know God better and, in return, you will know yourself better.

Once you acquire the habit of prayer, not only will you know Him better, you will love Him more for the life he has given you. You will also slowly realize that you will want to serve Him. For when you pray, pray not to God to do your will, but pray to accept His will. Turn your life's journey over to God. He knows, and has always known, the path you should take.

Plus this "turning over" of control will take an enormous weight off your shoulders.

I wrote earlier in this book that God lives in your subconscious. Through private prayer you will dig deep inside yourself and find Him there waiting. He is *always* with you.

Even at the busiest times, when your mind is full of a thousand thoughts, and anxiety is at its peak, you will feel His presence and you will be aware of an incredible inner strength as a powerful voice reminds you, *"I am here, and you are not alone."*

The question now is, "How do I pray?" I pray in many ways, always alone with God. I pray softly in bed each night or I pray through writing in my daily journal. If you remember, back in chapter one I wrote, *"I know there is a God! Today is a revelation. Every prayer I have ever made has been answered."* From that day forth I have believed completely in the existence of God, and that belief has come through prayer. Here are some examples of how I have incorporated prayer in my journal writing:

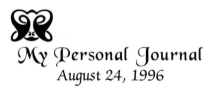

My Personal Journal
August 24, 1996

'We try and give our whole lives to God and do His will in every respect. Herein lies our spiritual growth. . . . herein lies our future . . . an ever-widening horizon.'

"I pray tonight that I may follow the inner urgings of my soul . . . What are those inner urgings? Love, compassion, understanding, patience, forgiveness and a deeper relationship with God.

I felt His incredible grace yesterday, and I saw His beauty of creation today in the face of my son and the beauty of nature around me.

I pray, Lord, that my heart opens completely, and that I am not afraid to reveal my inner, loving self. I remember several months back I prayed you would show me what true love is, and you have answered my prayer in a number of ways. Thank you so much Lord . . . I feel your presence now, and it is phenomenal."

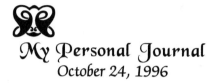

My Personal Journal
October 24, 1996

"I decided it was time to make a trip to the beach . . . my conscious mind seemed to be a little cluttered, but I made it all the same.

It's a warm night with a warm breeze. The full moon has risen high overhead, illuminating the ocean and the old wooden pier. The water sparkles in the moonlight as I make my way to God's waiting boat. I notice along the way one of the pier's lamps is out...maybe that signifies our power outage. (Our power has been out several days because of a freak heavy and wet early season snowstorm.)

The first thing I ask God is, 'What do I do next?' He says, 'Nothing, have patience, I will guide you. Chris, you are too much in a hurry. Events will happen when the time is right. Isn't that what happened with your son Taylor?' I said, 'Yes Lord...my life is in your hands. Help me to let go of control and have patience. Fill me with love and help me share it with others. Rid me of my anger or help me to understand it. Thanks for helping me discover all I have in the past six or seven months.'

'Trust in me, Chris.' 'I do Lord, I do.'

I wanted to pray for faith, but I realized my faith is already secure. 'Thank you for life, Lord . . . Thank you for love.'

'Taylor's smile is a gift . . . he is a gift . . . my wife is a gift . . . Thank you Lord . . . Continue to smile down upon us.'"

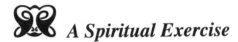

My Personal Journal
October 21, 1996

"Right now it is gently raining...another awesome sound . . . Thank you Lord for life and all its wonders . . . Keep me going in the right direction, break down my inner walls and make me vulnerable, open to all life has to offer . . . fill me with love, and let me share myself and that love. I have no control over the future, but that is okay, because it is in your guiding hands."

And that is where it should be.

A Spiritual Exercise

How to Pray

What do you want from prayer in your life? Get a piece of paper and answer these questions:

1. I want to feel love . . . how?

2. I want passion to express itself in my life . . . in which ways?

3. I want my ego boundaries to fall so I can get in touch with my inner self . . . so I can become . . .

4. I want to learn to surrender and become vulnerable . . . to improve what?

5. I want to have a closer relationship with God . . . in order to accomplish what?

6. I want my true self to emerge and stop letting my ego do the talking . . . why?

7. I want love to renew . . .

8. I want love to inspire . . .

9. I want to oust all fear from my life . . .

10. I want to harmonize differences . . . with whom?

Answer these questions and incorporate them into prayer. For example:

I want to feel love all the time, and act on it. I pray the Lord opens my heart and soul to love, and I may have the courage and inspiration to act on it.

Try this for several weeks and I promise you will begin to see the positive results in your daily life, and with this you will begin to have an increased faith or trust in God and the people in your daily life.

chapter eight

Faith

I bid to find on nature's path or midnight sky above
a mysterious force that "I's" are surely blind.
Is the answer sweet and light as the peaceful
   flight of a dove,
or must the mind, unwind, the scattering beliefs
   of the deepest kind?

Religion fosters believers to sanctimoniously be
in touch with a complete wholeness just out of grasp.
In hope of a glimpse, a serene light that mostly alludes
   the "I's" that see
until near death comes with a few final rasps.

Yet, the greater the struggle, the closer we come
to heaven's gate, even locked, footfalls can be heard.
We only need our doubts to succumb,
for angels' wings beat triumph, horns sound, and God's
   passionate word

will live as eternal as man needs
the purpose to proceed.

Chris Snyder
April 1997

To put it simply, the sonnet above describes faith as a belief in something we can not see or hear. But as we struggle with everyday life and our true selves, that faith or trust becomes stronger in either someone close to us or God. I believe faith lives deep inside us. But we question that faith always because of the tragedies we see and hear about or are happening to us. As I have discovered love and God, my faith has logically increased. Not just faith in God's existence, but faith in other people. I view people as naturally good, however, many make the wrong choices. Whether it be from a conscious or unconscious motivation.

My faith in the Lord was not always there. It has taken me a long time to reach that level. For example:

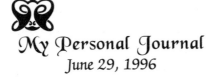

My Personal Journal
June 29, 1996

"I am so quick to find fault with others and God. I continue to need to work on having faith and being patient. I believe if I can get to that point, my own life and spirituality would be enriched in return.

Now back to what Jesus said, 'Love the Lord your God with all your heart . . .' Up until just lately I have been extremely skeptical as to God's existence. I do believe now, more than ever, in His existence . . . not only within me, but all around me. But there is a part of me that can not even comprehend loving God with all my heart. Don't get me wrong, I love God more and more every day for everything He has given me and my family. But is that enough?"

I now believe that is not enough. You must love God with all your heart and find and cultivate the faith that lives deep inside you.

My Personal Journal
July 23, 1996

"There seems to be this small part, deep inside me, that I have uncovered or am in the process of discovering. Faith, strength and stability emanate from this area. I seem not to worry at all when decisions come through this 'faith-touched' place. Actually, on the average, I seem to worry less about the circumstances I have the least control over. I still push myself to the limit to get too much accomplished, but there is a new part of me that is so full of faith, strength and confidence.

It's like a patch of fresh green grass in a newly found land that I thought didn't exist. I'm not saying it's the end to all my problems, but it's an undiluted thing when it pops up and knows the correct answer without a doubt; without reservation. However I discovered it, I pray to you, Lord, it stays with me and continues to grow. It is a dazzling feeling and presence, and lately faith seems to be there when I need it most."

Faith, love and God will always be there when you need them most, or just a little bit. Remember, when times are very tough, think to yourself, "I have faith." Because the one thing you should know is you have already been through the worst, and lived through it.

If you possess great faith and love, even if you are not aware of it, you also possess spirituality. And with that spirituality will come a journey to a deeper understanding of yourself and the spinning world around you.

chapter nine

Patience

In this fast-paced, *no-time-to-sit-down,* frenzied world the word patience and its meaning have been lost. I pray often for patience because without it I find that I am just living in the future, not in the moment of now. To sit back and have patience is really arduous work. You would think it should be easy, but it is certainly not. You must have strong faith and the conscious realization you can't control every situation. You can only do your very best, and if that is not enough, it is not meant to be.

You must remind yourself, daily, to have patience. Patience *is* a virtue, and it is also a learned quality. I am sure you have heard the saying, "Good things come to those who wait." Well, that saying could not be further from the truth.

Without patience in life, you find yourself spending enormous energy waiting for the "phone call to come" or "the package to arrive." And that phone call or package may never come.

Early in my television career, I sent out hundreds of resume tapes, and just *sat by the phone* waiting for a news director to call and offer me a great job. I spent way too much time *waiting* when I could have been doing something much more productive like eating. With that constant, obsessional waiting came an increase in anxiety and the whole day was lost.

Over time, I realized when you least expect it, the thing you want dearly will usually occur. It just takes a deep belief in yourself and a whole lot of patience.

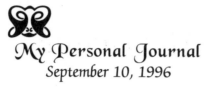

My Personal Journal
September 10, 1996

"A voice just rang out in my head, 'Patience, it will happen.' I believe that voice. It seems to always know. In my journey I feel like I am headed up a winding mountain road lined with tall, beautiful fur trees, and there is a big bend up ahead...I can't see where I am going . . . 'Patience', that voice says again.

Lord, I pray for patience once again tonight . . . patience with myself and others tomorrow. Continue to fill me with love. Good night."

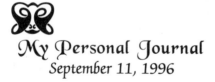

My Personal Journal
September 11, 1996

"I thought I would take a trip to that special place inside me last night. It was a tough night to get there. My conscious mind appeared cloudy . . . like I was caught in a thunderstorm. But I eventually made it, and was surprised by how well I felt on the beach. The moon had already risen, and the pale light reflected beautifully off the delicately rolling waves. The rhythm of the waves and the temperate whisper of the sea grass were relaxing at once. I just felt like lying on the sandy beach, and letting go of myself. As I relaxed, I noticed a ship far out in the sea of my unconsciousness, and I wondered what it could mean

. . . what could it be carrying? . . . where could it be going? This was the first time I had seen a ship out on the ocean.

A few minutes passed, and I decided to walk out onto the pier. The cool ocean spray, full of salt, felt refreshing when it hit my face.

When I got to God's waiting boat, He immediately said, 'Patience. Have patience . . . believe in Me and in your heart.' I said, 'Can I open my eyes and will you give me some sort of sign?' The Lord answered, 'Your faith is wavering, but open your eyes and you will see me all around you.'

And you know, He was right.

Thank you, Lord . . . for my wonderful life, wife and son. Be with me always and keep me on the right path in life. I have been spoiled by your grace lately . . . I have taken it for granted. Help me to see it more again. Remind me of the value of patience and continue filling me with love. Help me to release anger, and bring down my ego walls that hide my true self."

My true self. What an astounding spiritual journey this is. As I continue on the path, life, love and a deepening spirituality slowly reveal, like a sunrise, even more of their precious powers.

chapter ten

Spirituality

*Yet it is obvious that the soul, seat of the deepest
emotions, can benefit greatly from the gifts of a vivid
spiritual life and can suffer when it is deprived of them.*
                                    Thomas Moore, **Care of the Soul**

I wrote a few chapters back that the essence of love is far too deep and encompassing to give you a fully adequate definition. As I begin this chapter on spirituality, I feel I am faced with the same dilemma. How can I sufficiently define spirituality? Maybe in the beginning it is best to first break the word down to *spirit.* Spirit is defined as "The vital essence of man, considered divine in origin; the part of a human being characterized by personality and self-consciousness; the Holy Ghost; the creative power of God." I give credence to the *spirit* living in the subconscious where God, and innocent and pure love, also exist. With God is the creative power of God and the poetic power to start you on the genuine journey of spirituality. But first there has to be a spark to start a spiritual fire. That *spark* ignites in people at various points in their lives. It could be the death of a loved one, the ultimate fear of death itself, or simply the consciousness your life needs new deeper meaning and direction. Unfortunately, in most people, the journey never begins at all, usually due to fear. It is easier to live simply and in accordance with what society calls *normal.*

The fear in spirituality is the pain that accompanies the tremendous growth necessary for a spiritual journey to begin. Pain occurs when we start to think and look deeply within ourselves and confront our hidden flaws.

I am not quite certain when exactly my spiritual journey began. It could have been in May of 1987 when I quit drinking or, more likely, it was in May of 1996 when I began to consciously realize there is much, much more to life than just simplistic thinking, and I desired to look deeper within to find my true self and my always present, but hidden, spirituality or faith in God's existence.

Faith in the Creator's existence did not come overnight. When I quit drinking I had prayed to God often to help me stop, but I did not have that much faith in His divine existence. The faith grew slowly over the years from constant prayer and meditation until I, with the help of Jo Jeanne, began to see God's grace and hear Him speak to me in my heart. Since then my constant Companion on the spiritual path has been God, but once again I say I am not trying to convert you. You can certainly be a confirmed atheist and still be highly spiritual.

Spirituality begins in the conscious mind. If we do not get *stuck* in our conscious or ego development, then there is a chance that we will begin to look deeper and understand better the *light* inside ourselves. When I say *stuck* I mean in one of the two early forms of ego development. In psychology the ego is divided into three growth phases. The first being in childhood when the ego is limited to just early emotions that have limited effects. The second phase is during adolescence. For the first time teenagers can observe themselves being happy, sad or angry when they are feeling a certain way. They can choose to deal with these emotions or *stick them under the rug*. This is also an obvious time of rebellion. The young adult may self-consciously try on different identities, change hairstyles and dress and behave radically. Adolescents can become overwhelmed by being self-conscious about their appearance and constantly comparing themselves to family and friends. This self-consciousness is painful, and many get *stuck* in this second phase of ego development because of the intense *growing pains*. The few lucky ones move on to the third stage and begin seeing life in a quite different light. They are able to realize their flaws, integrate them into their lives, and think more deeply about themselves and their reactions to life's numerous situations. Strong emotions become bearable and often sought after for experience and growth. *Thinking* takes on a new meaning. No longer is simple thinking the answer. I remember hearing a phrase at some point in high school . . . the abbreviation for the phrase is K.I.S.S. Which stands for *Keep It Simple Stupid*. That phrase should actually be changed to *It's Stupid to Keep it Simple*. If you keep it simple when you are thinking about problems, you are going to come up with a simple solution and miss many of the different aspects of a problem that deserves a deeper, more complete answer. We must take the time and make the complete effort and face the pain involved, think deeply and fully contemplate our answers. It is conscious hard work. Many people do not take the time to think deeply. It's much easier and more painless to just *Keep it Simple Stupid*.

If you are on a spiritual path or just starting a journey, you must continue to grow, and your conscious mind (ego) must also continue to grow. And as you look deeply, face the larger responsibilities that come with growth and answer the problems you use to avoid or put off, you can become more open to your unconscious where serenity, bliss and God exist.

> *"From the one who has been entrusted with much, much more will be asked."*
>
> **Luke 12:48**

It is a wonderful thing to be in touch with the real you and God.

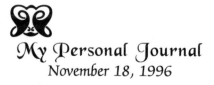

My Personal Journal
November 18, 1996

"I feel I have spent my whole life looking for love. I love you, Lord. You are with me. Show me your will, Lord. I will follow. Love is more than just a feeling. It is surrendering. It is self-

sacrifice. I will give my life to you, Lord. I will give my life for Kris and Taylor. I will move mountains if you tell me to try, Lord. Love is powerful . . . it is also powerless. Love requires self-discipline. You must give all you have to give. Open my heart fully, Lord. Free my spirit and let me share it with others. I am a vessel to be filled with love. Love, honor and obey . . . respect one another for that is all we have under God."

I learned a long time ago to put my life in God's hands. This is an awesome responsibility for God and yourself. If you are giving your life to God, He is going to ask more and more of you because along that spiritual path, the more you grow, the more responsible you will be. You will become more responsible, because you have been touched by God. You will begin to see, understand and feel on a *higher* level. Your responsibility will be to share your increased awareness and love with others, even people whom you have had conflict with. You must share the **goodness.** Actually, you **will want** to share. On numerous occasions, I have wanted desperately to talk in person or call someone close and share the *wealth* because that is now what I have: a powerful wealth of deeper understanding, peace, hope and love.

> *"I feel it's been awhile since I have written in a deep manner. Maybe it was to stay away from the growth and change that occurs so the anxiety would also stay away.*
>
> *I know we must come to terms with change in our lives, which requires continual adjustments in the way or depth we think and behave. Change to me feels almost like dying. It would be much easier to stay comfortable with where I am, but in reality I would go crazy if I didn't continue to change and grow."*

You are by now thinking, How do I start this spiritual journey? It may sound like it is difficult to begin. It does take work, conscious work, but the *letting go* of troubling thoughts and looking deeper within yourself increases the joy, peace and hope you will find.

Peace and spirituality go hand in hand. You will be amazed and thankful for the increased peace and tranquility you will encounter.

 *A Spiritual Exercise*

Spirituality

Close your eyes and take a few deep breaths. Imagine you are in your conscious mind just floating gently like you are in warm water. Begin to look around and see if you notice a little opening to another place within you. If this doesn't happen, don't worry. Do not try and make it happen . . . just let it happen. My little opening, as I have mentioned before, is a hole with shards of brilliant light emanating from deep within. As I slowly enter this hole, I am gently pulled downward until I land on a beautiful beach at night. The sand is warm, and the full moon is rising out of a placid ocean. Its glorious light grows wider and wider until it hits the beach. I usually sit there for a moment, listening to the mesmerizing music the breeze plays through the sea grass. I feel calm and very peaceful.

In front of me is the wooden pier. It juts out over the ocean and makes a right turn. I can see God's waiting boat floating there. I feel safe here, and never want to leave, but I make my way to the pier. Tall and curved at the top, rusty lamps cast circular yellowish light along my path over the pastoral wooden slats. With every step, I grow increasingly calm.

As I walk up to the boat I can see God is radiating His own soft light. At this point I feel I can ask Him any question I want, or He will start the discussion.

My Personal Journal
September 17, 1996

"As I reached God's boat He did say, 'Have patience, but you have forgotten something you learned long ago. Live one day at a time, but for you it would be better to live one second at a time. Chris, . . . Live in the **Precious Present.** (Another good book by the way.) I will take care of the future for you, and as to the past, learn from it, but let it go. One second at a time, Chris. Also let go of some of your control . . . You come to my boat because I steer and control the direction we travel . . . let me show you the way, and if you can, let me control your life.' (That was hard to write down.)

And the Lord said, 'That's a hard thing to do.'

Lord, thank you for my life . . . my destiny is in your hands...guide me and take me down the right path in life. Thank you for love, Lord . . . thank you for my incredible life.

The stars were stunning as I looked to the sky. Like diamonds resting on a black velvet background.

Good night, Lord . . . Good night, Kris and Taylor. I love you."

I can't emphasize enough how extremely important it is to find a *special place* inside yourself and then write often about what happens there. It doesn't need to be a beach. It can be any place you choose.

I have found my spiritual beach to be the cure, and answer, for whatever is bothering me. And when I return the world looks a little different, a little brighter. Even as I type this late at night, I feel good in my heart about experiencing this again with you, and with God.

chapter eleven

Grace

As your inward growth and spirituality continues to blossom, you will begin to catch glimpses of a powerful force that originates outside of our human consciousness, but is influenced by our deepening consciousness. We can not touch this force, and there is no way to measure its intensity. But it is strong and it's all around and inside of us.

I am talking about the grace of God or, in other words, God's infinite and powerful love. Why does God touch us with His grace? Because He wants us to grow. But what is the goal of this growth? I have come to the conclusion that God wants us to become Himself. God is the ultimate goal of growth. It is God who is the source of grace, and who is the final destination.

This idea may sound impossible, but actually it is quite simple. Because if we believe in this theory, as I now fully do, grace and God demand all we have to give. This is an awesome responsibility. It means we must always strive to grow, love and become better individuals. It requires us to think deeply, constantly and hard. We must give all we can to this endeavor. But most of us do not want to take on this responsibility. We don't want to work that hard. Life is tough enough. As long as we believe godhood is unattainable, we do not have to worry about our spiritual growth. It's our way out.

Our spiritual growth ends here. But how can we ignore this power? How can we ignore God's grace? By giving it another name like luck? I don't think so. As we continue along our spiritual journey, we will begin to see God's grace and we will feel its tremendous love.

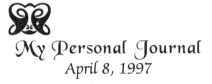

My Personal Journal
April 8, 1997

"I am not quite sure what is happening to me. I feel so in touch with my inner self . . . so in touch with God. It is almost overwhelming. Last night I went to an "aftercare" meeting at Shawnee Mission Medical Center, and spoke about more than I realized I knew. I believe God was speaking through me. I was there for a definite reason. I was there to help a man through God's grace. This man (I will call Mark) had just relapsed a few days after going through extensive treatment for alcoholism. I could see . . . I could feel his emptiness and pain. I could feel Mark was not even close to his inner self. He was just treading on the surface of a deep and frightening ocean. He was lost. I used to be lost, but I have found some of the many pieces. Not a great amount, but enough for me to catch a glimpse of God and His heartwarming grace. I spoke of emptiness, love, spirituality, structure, grace and God. How I could and still can feel God's immense love and close presence. If this is just a small, tiny piece of God I am feeling, He is truly magnificent. I can hardly handle this tiny piece. How extraordinary the wholeness of God must be. His presence is so deeply filled with strength, filling light, peace and love (grace). How can I explain His wholeness? Imagine the universe, only larger."

This may sound incredible, but I now see God's grace on a daily basis. Whether it be in my son's innocent smile, my wife's soft touch, or even making it through a string of green lights when I am late on my way to work. It is grace. When you hear people say, "I was at the right place at the right time," that is grace, not just luck.

I remember several years ago I was at a major crossroad in my life. I had just been laid off from my job at a radio station in St. Louis, when my mother suggested I call around and try to find an internship in television news. She had always believed I was meant for TV. It was late August, though, and by this time all intern spots for the fall were already filled. Especially at the number one station in the market, KSDK. But I thought, "What do I have to lose?" I called the station, and by the grace of God an intern had *just quit that morning!* After I told her about my radio experience, the intern director said, "Come on down this afternoon, and we will see if you meet the requirements." The meeting was quick, and I was accepted. I clearly remember the intern director saying, "Right time, right place. You got a big break. Make the most of it." And I did. Six months later, after some hard grunt work and showing I truly cared, KSDK helped me to get my first job in television news. It was a small station in north Texas, but it was a start. Six years later, I have moved up the ladder, and I am now working at a station in my hometown of Kansas City. What an incredible turn around! I have a great job, a wonderful wife and son, and a much closer relationship with my mother and God. What more could anyone ask?

chapter twelve

God

I am just sitting here on a clear, warm night attempting to think what to write about in this chapter on God. A little strange, don't you think? I have filled numerous journals, and most of this book, with pages about a loving and passionate God, and I can't find a starting point for this chapter. The words, "God is the answer," continue repeating in my mind. Maybe that is a starting point, but how can I define God in just one chapter of a small book. God is too immense to be limited to any chapter, or a book, even the Bible.

God is the beginning, and the end. The Alpha and Omega. God is *the answer.* He has been the answer. He has been the answer in every struggle I have had throughout my life. In the end, the answer always comes back to God.

God is love, and love is God. God's grace is shown in our lives daily. We just have to look a little closer to see it. You may be wondering, "Where am I going with this? Don't I have a personal journal entry I could use?" I'm not sure which one. I'm not sure why I am having trouble. It may be too big of a challenge for me to explain to you the utter immenseness of God. I guess I am asking for faith for just a moment so I can search deeply for more information. I feel certain something significant will happen.

*   *   *   *   *

(The next morning . . .)

And it did. Overnight, my twenty-one month old son had a severe asthmatic reaction to an unknown allergen. Taylor was awake most of the night crying. Early this morning, we took him to the pediatrician, and Taylor spent almost six hours in her office. He was nearly admitted to the hospital. What does this have to do with God? I prayed often, and I thank God Taylor is alive, but honestly I am angry at the Lord for this happening. I have realized how dearly and deeply I love my son who, I believe, is a gift from God. A gift almost returned. But during this traumatic time, I felt an absence of God for the first time in a long time. I'm not sure why. It's hard to explain. Possibly this feeling or sense of loss is what St. John of the Cross, in the sixteenth century, said is "the dark night of the soul." A point where God seems to be totally absent. I had a deep sense that God, who is usually present and active at every moment of my life, had just disappeared. Or maybe it is the realization of the frailty of life and the finality of death. We are so close to life and death at the same time. So I hope the pattern holds true with God. We are always close to Him in both life and death.

My faith has been definitely tested, and in some aspects it has failed. My faith in God wavered, but I realize that is a part of being human. That is not to say I have become faithless. Who is to say a mature faith doesn't sometimes need testing. Faith is meant to be tested throughout our lives. That is how it ultimately grows stronger and stronger. In the Bible, God tested Abraham to the point he was truly committed to sacrifice, on an altar, the son he deeply loved to God. If that was God's will, Abraham accepted it with much pain and sorrow, no matter what the finality of his actions. When that traumatic point occurred, God knew Abraham, in his soul, had ultimate love and faith for God. God stopped Abraham from sacrificing his son, and Abraham sacrificed a lamb instead.

A true test of faith. It is how we respond to these tests that shapes our relationship with God. I now hope my faith in God has grown stronger. I feel it has.

But once again I am faced with the question that we all ask, "Why would a God of love let this happen, especially to a young child?" My heart cries out deeply in pain for the suffering Taylor must be going through. I know my child did not die, and there are many children every day that do, but why? It is simply not enough to say, "God works in mysterious ways." I can come up with no answer that contains complete certainty. I can just theorize that possibly God has to work under rules He created. I believe God gave us "free will" and by doing so we are free to choose good or evil. And since both those forces are now free to roam about our world, God has to live under the rules He set forth, no matter how much it might hurt me, you or even God.

chapter thirteen

The Moment of Now and Peace

I believe strongly that God lives in *the moment of now.* There is no other way for Him to live. He is constantly watching us grow, nudging us in the right direction by His grace, testing our faith, and listening to our prayers.

I believe we must also live in *the moment of now.* Not in the past or in the future. The past can be learned from, but if you are not careful, painful past experiences can cloud how you perceive and handle events in the present.

On the other hand, living in the future is impossible. You can believe all your future plans (I like to call them dominoes) are set up, but one tiny deviation or unexpected event can knock all the dominos down.

Have you ever tried to live in the moment of now? It is a tough, but rewarding thing to accomplish. Your thoughts continually wander into both the past and what effects the past will have on your future.

If you are able to live in the moment of now, it will feel as though time has stopped. Everything you view takes on clearer meaning. You begin to notice the small, special, good things in life. You feel at peace with the world around you. But be careful, the moment of now can slip away quickly. Your mind (ego) is trained to think about what you need to achieve, and we begin to feel guilty we are wasting time enjoying the moment of now. But the best things in life happen in the present.

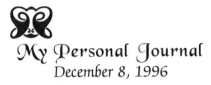

My Personal Journal
December 8, 1996

"The last couple of days have been good ones. I have been at peace. It is as I'm not used to feeling this peaceful, so it is a new experience. I have not been writing as much lately, so I am a little mad at myself. I don't feel as open and in touch when I do not write, but for some reason I haven't wanted to write lately.

On Friday, I went to the University of Kansas and enrolled for the spring semester. I am excited to start school again in January, and I have a clear cut plan for the future. Maybe that is part of the problem. I have been living too much in the future lately. I need to remind myself more often to live in the moment of now.

A couple of days ago, I wrote, 'Back to the basics . . .' That is so true. Keep it simple, Chris, and live by the basics and what you have written in the past.

With my new schedule, I find myself with so much more leisure time. Time I have been using to rest a lot and run errands I have needed to accomplish for some time.

Life is going well, but something is missing, or is it? I guess for so long I have been living with anxiety, and now that it is gone, I feel sort of empty . . . not really empty, but different. My conscious mind wants to explore and rest at the same time!

After rereading what I just wrote, I still can't completely put a finger on it, but maybe there is not much to put a finger on except for a new-found peace and less anxiety. I think I will let this roll over in my mind for awhile, and see what I think later. Then, I will just let it go.

I believe I need a moment with nature. I have not written about nature recently. But I think that is partially because I am so much of a warm weather person. There I go again, living in the future. The moment of now is so tough to stay in!

As I write tonight, the more at peace I feel . . . that's a good sign. Thank you, Lord, for all you have given me. Keep me on the journey, and show me Your will. I *will* follow. Let my emotions flow like a mountain stream, and let me recognize and share them with others. Break down my inner walls, and let my soul dance freely with You, love, peace, and all life has to offer."

Becoming closer to God has brought me amazing peace and hope. *It can happen to you!* Just live in *the moment of now*, and develop a relationship with yourself, the world around you, and God.

chapter fourteen

Thoughts on an Afterlife

Critical rationalism has apparently eliminated, along with so many other mythic conceptions, the idea of life after death. This could only have happened because nowadays most people identify themselves almost exclusively with their consciousness, and imagine that they are only what they know about themselves.

(Jung, Carl. **Memories, Dreams, Reflections**)

In other words, we are extremely narrowminded, fearful and believe in only what we can see, touch or understand. Most of us have no understanding of an afterlife because we have not experienced this transition from physical life to death. The small group of people who understand have a different outlook on life after death because of either near-death experiences, premonitions, or dreams of a family member's death.

As I move along on my spiritual journey, my awareness of death grows, but so does my knowledge of an afterlife. As I said earlier, "I know there is a God." So it logically stands to reason I know there is an afterlife. I use the word *know*, because to just believe would mean I have doubts. I have no doubts. What exactly occurs in this afterlife, I am not sure. "If there is something we cannot know, we must necessarily abandon it as an intellectual problem. For example, I do not know for what reason the universe has come into being, and shall never know. Therefore I must drop this question as a scientific or intellectual problem. But if an idea about it is offered to me—in dreams or mythic traditions—I ought to take note of it. I even ought to build up a conception on the basis of such hints, even though it will forever remain a hypothesis which I know cannot be proved" (302).

I believe I have personal proof of life after death, but before I get to that let me give you some background on my religious upbringing.

I was brought up in a family that did not attend church on a regular basis. We went randomly or on special holidays like Christmas and Easter. But aside from that, we did not attend weekly.

Earlier in my life, I rationalized that religion and God were just a means of comforting people about their eventual death. They lived and coped more sensibly, felt better, and were more at peace with their existence if they believed there was life after death. My intellectual rationalizations and beliefs were transformed, suddenly, in May 1996. To say the least, my consciousness did a complete somersault. I discovered my hidden, but strong, spirituality, and a deep knowledge of God's existence. I was not even considering the possibility of an afterlife until a magical, deeply spiritual awakening happened one evening.

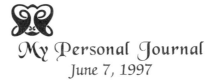

My Personal Journal
June 7, 1997

"I had an incredible, powerful and peaceful experience last night that I am not sure what to call. I do not want to say it was an 'out of body experience' because I am not sure that sounds correct.

It was about 8:20 pm, and I decided to take a nap for about an hour before the ten o'clock news. I was lying down on my back in a darkened 'green room' (a room in the television business we use for guests who are waiting to be on the air), but I never fell asleep. I am sure of this because I could still here the muffled sounds of the television station around me.

At first I decided to do an exercise I do often called 'letting go.' You take deep breaths, and with every one you take in, you let it fill your heart. This is so you can get in touch with your emotions. For a few minutes, I found this difficult to do because my mind kept interrupting me with thoughts of the future. When I was finally focused, I asked my heart to speak to me, and a few thoughts and stored-up emotions came to the forefront of my mind that I took a look at then 'let go.'

Then, suddenly, I felt God's strong presence, and my body felt like it was expanding, and my mind was completely opening up. My ego was released, and I saw a brilliant, bright light in my mind. A light so powerful and pure I wanted to approach it, but I could only get so close before I was held back. I felt at total peace and extremely safe. I asked God what was happening, but I can not recall what He said. At this time, I felt like my body and mind were turning into complete energy, and my body was taking on an enormous, long, almost flat shape. At moments, I felt like I could almost totally let go, but something was holding me back from doing so. I kept asking God if I could just see a glimpse of heaven, but He told me, 'No.' I felt so close to Heaven, but I could go no further. It was as if the clouds of heaven were just above me, but I couldn't quite reach them. I called for my grandmother, who had been on my mind lately, and her hand come down out of the clouds and touched my hand, just for a quick moment. It is an indescribable experience. I kept asking God to let me go further, but He would't let me. I had this tremendous feeling I did not want to return . . . return to life on earth.

At this time my body felt miles long, and energy, in waves, was flowing through it. I asked God to see Andy. Andy was my best friend's brother, who had died tragically long ago. It took some time, like he was coming from a great distance, but then some loving part of him was with me. I can't recall what we talked about, but the words, 'Don't worry,' remain in my mind. I say again, I am certain I was not dreaming because I could still faintly hear the sounds of channel five in the distance.

The strange thing I still remember is how long and stretched out my body felt, and how extremely open my spirit and soul were. And the feeling of turning into energy was very intense.

I just know I didn't want to leave this place because everything made sense to my soul. I felt so calm and safe.

After the experience was over, I felt a little angry and dumbfounded. I knew I should not feel angry, but I really did not want to leave, and I couldn't completely understand, but part of me knew I must return for my wife and son.

What exactly happened and why, I am not sure.

I think God said, 'It was not my time,' and my wife, Kris, said the same thing after I told her about the experience.

That experience was as real to me as the hot summer sun in August. I theorize it occurred because the more deeply in touch I become with my subconscious, the more free I (we) become from the constraints of time and space. There is another dimension to our lives we are just becoming aware of. "I have become convinced that at least a part of our psychic existence is characterized by a relativity of space and time. This relativity seems to increase, in the proportion to the distance from consciousness, to an absolute condition of timelessness and spacelessness" (305).

Many people have asked me why I consider death and life after death at the young age of thirty-one. As I have said before, I believe we must face death to become conscious of the contents that press upward from the depths of our unconscious. The unconscious, the spirit, the soul, know the answers because God lives in our subconscious. "But while the man who despairs marches towards nothingness, the one who has placed his faith in the archetype follows the tracks of life and lives right unto his death" (306).

A person should be able to say he or she has done his or her best to form a conception of life after death, or at least to create some image of it. Not to have done so is a vital loss. For to do so adds itself to our own individual life in order to make it more fulfilled.

*   *   *   *   *

So far, I have just addressed the fundamental viewpoints of the afterlife from a Christian aspect. A view that embodies self-knowledge as to the knowledge of God. What about the ideas and images concerning reincarnation? That is, the succession of birth and death is viewed as an endless cycle. Man is born, lives and gains knowledge and wisdom, and then dies, beginning from where he left off.

Today, there is a lot of discussion about "old" souls and "new" souls. Many believe the "old" souls have been reborn a number of times, and are close to what the Buddhists call "nirvana." That is to say, the soul has reached a certain stage of complete understanding. It then would no longer have to return to earth. The soul would vanish from this three-dimensional world, and remain in nirvana.

I can imagine I have lived in previous centuries, and not answered the questions I was supposed to, and when I died, my accomplishments followed me into the next life. But that brings up the Buddhist view of *karma* . . . is it personal or not? Do we carry over our achievements to the next life or just begin all over? That question was never answered by Buddha, and remains a mystery.

Another thought I would like to review is what occurs when the soul reaches nirvana? Since there is theoretically no need for further learning, does it just exist in some form, floating about in eternity? Or at some point, somewhere in the distant future, does the soul fall out of nirvana because the world has progressed to where the once fully complete soul once again has questions to be answered? This is a question I do not know the answer to. And maybe it is better that I don't. If I had that answer, why would I continue to strive for significant knowledge of life and the afterlife?

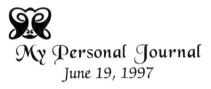

My Personal Journal
June 19, 1997

"Everyday I discover there is so much to learn about ourselves and the way that learning reflects itself in our daily interactions with people and with life itself. I also acknowledge, though, we don't have to figure it all out. That would be impossible, and what point would there be to life if we knew all the answers?

I understand, on a scientific basis, why the sun rises every morning, but why was it set up that way from the start? For eventual human existence? We are so bounded and taught there are constraints of a beginning and an end. But how did the universe start? How did God come to be? Was there another God before Him? If so, how did He come to be? The theory of the "Big Bang" is quite intriguing. It could be rationalized as a starting point, but who or what organized the particles necessary for life in the beginning? If the scientific principle is true that energy cannot be created or destroyed, how did the energy of the universe come to be created?

Man certainly did not create the earth, galaxies, and universe. Man did not even create love. There has to be a reason, a force, and for those who say, "There is no reason, it just happened by random chance," that is a cop-out. That is simplistic thinking

. . . ignoring the far reaching possibilities of creation whether it be from the Christian viewpoint or Buddhist's religious ideas.

What would life be like if we knew all the answers? Answers are what we search for everyday, whether it be on a work level or spiritual level. And to ignore the bigger questions just because we can't comprehend them, or choose not to, is fear. Fear we may have it all wrong, and the simple answer is all around us . . . God.

Search for God deep in yourself . . . He is there, and He will answer most of the questions you need to know. But some will remain unanswered because we must continue to search on our own. That is how we spiritually grow. But when that growing is complete, what is next? And why is there such an insurmountable boundary between the dead and living? Is it the ultimate test of faith? I believe so, but I can only speculate. God is the only one who truly knows."

Roadblocks to
Spirituality

chapter fifteen

Anxiety

Everybody at one time or another experiences anxiety, only a small, but growing, percentage become impaired by it. A recent study on the prevalence of mental disorders revealed that anxiety disorders were the most prevalent group of psychiatric diagnoses affecting almost 13% of the population *(Essential Psychopathology and Its Treatment,* Maxmen and Ward, 245). Those disorders run the gamut from panic to social phobias to generalized and chronic anxiety.

Anxiety in moderation can be highly useful since optimal learning and adaptation to a variety of problems occur at a mid level rather than high or low levels of anxiety. "While moderate levels of anxiety may be normal and adaptive, the ability to vary anxiety levels in response to different situations is also desirable. Most people have a characteristic range of anxiety responses that is relatively fixed and can be viewed as a personality trait. This is called 'trait anxiety.' In clinical settings, when trait anxiety is uniformly high and maladaptive, it is called *chronic anxiety*" (245).

For an extended period of my life, anxiety was maladaptive and not conducive to spiritual growth. You can not have such growth when a majority of your energy is utilized for coping with acute anxiety. As I mentioned before, early in college I was first struck by a panic attack in the middle of the night. People who have never suffered from one may find them hard to understand. Panic attacks are excruciating, painful experiences that come on suddenly without reason, where you ultimately feel you are going to die. "'Worse than anything at Aushwitz is how a concentration-camp survivor described her panic attacks" (251). After the initial attack numerous others followed. In between my attacks my anxiety grew from fear of having another attack. Thus, I formed a chronic anxiety disorder that for years became a daily part of my life. It was not until some eight years later, after the damage was done, that I sought treatment and was diagnosed. It was a great relief to find out I was not going crazy. Over time, therapy sessions and medication produced fabulous results. I have come to find anxiety is motivational and needed. It is sad, however, that most people with anxiety disorders do not seek treatment because they see themselves as weak. Not wanting to admit to themselves and others they have a problem that would ruin the image they have worked hard to create. Treatment is proven highly effective, and without it, less than twenty-five percent of these people fully recover. In general, the earlier in life these patients seek treatment, the better the long-term outcome. Thus, early detection definitely matters.

I now see my anxiety as a blessing. Without the anguishing experience, I would have never begun a spiritual journey. It was the motivational force to look deeper within myself and find the answers. And hidden beneath the anxiety, I have found love, compassion, a solid belief in God, and the overwhelming desire to write this book and share my experiences. My hope is that just one person will read this book, realize what is intruding on his or her inward growth, seek treatment and begin a spiritual journey. I have and continue to experience the ultimate wonders of life, and have come to terms with and learned to better understand my anxiety. I believe that God gives us all a cross to bear, and this one is mine.

With the heavy fog of anxiety lifted, I am now able to feel and express emotions such as love, and think on a deeply inward level. Thinking deeply is essential to understanding yourself and your relationships with others, including God.

"Recognize what is before your eyes, and what is hidden will be revealed to you."

Gospel of Thomas

With recognition comes joy and hope, but with maladaptive anxiety comes no joy, hope or spiritual journey.

There are a number of theories that focus on the causes of anxiety. These include the Psychodynamic theory which postulates that anxiety results from a failure to repress painful memories, impulses or thoughts. Secondly, behavior theories explain anxiety as a conditioned response that grows in intensity over time. Finally, biological theories maintain that anxiety originates in the brain, which in turn produces bodily symptoms such as sweating, rapid breathing, a racing heart, weak muscles, etc . . . And in turn, these physical sensations increase the anxiety felt in the brain. So a vicious circle is started.

During the past twenty-five years a number of advances in the treatment of anxiety have been made. Most include the latest in medication with some form of therapeutic treatment. Finding the right psychologist or psychiatrist is essential. Look for someone who specializes in anxiety and ask if they include spirituality in their treatment. A number of books published recently have discussed spirituality as the missing component in therapeutic relationships. I agree. With spirituality comes love, and a loving relationship is necessary for successful treatment. This comes from both personal experience and my reading. Learning to love and understand yourself is imperative for healing and becoming able to love and share with others. Once you are able to share, a personal form of therapy begins, and if you include with this the art of keeping a daily journal, you will begin to find what triggers your anxiety. My triggers are responsibility and change (I used personal journal entries in the chapter on "Spirituality" to discuss that anxiety).

Whatever is the cause for your chronic or acute anxiety does not really matter at the beginning. That answer will come if you face the problem instead of just *living with it*. Why, in this book, does it usually come down to *facing the problem?* Most likely, because that is what we ultimately avoid . . . problems. It is much easier to suppress than address. Address your pain and problems and *let them go.* Open space in your heart and soul for more positive emotions such as love. As they say, "Getting there (the journey) is half the fun."

 *Anxiety*

A Mind Purification Exercise

Through my personal experiences with acute anxiety, I have learned several ways of coping with the haunting problem. The first, and most important is exercise. Whether it be jogging, high speed walking, a fifteen-minute work-out on a stair-stepper machine or just a walk in the park, exercising three times a week, or especially after a stressful day, can be anxiety releasing.

Along with exercise, some variety of meditation or biofeedback can be extremely invaluable. I have found one form that works wonders for me. And I am going to share it with you.

Find a time when you are not going to be bothered for at least a half an hour. Turn off the telephone, and let the answering machine take the calls for you. If that makes you still feel anxious, pull the plug on the phone completely. Find your favorite comfortable chair or lie down in bed in a darkened room. Just relax for a few minutes. Then start taking deep breaths using your diaphragm. That is, make your lower abdominal muscles rise and fall with every breath. Close your eyes and take five slow, deep breaths, in through your nose, and out through your mouth. This signals your brain to automatically relax. Keep breathing deep, and begin to imagine you are lying on a warm beach at sunrise. Listen to the soothing, cascading waves. As the sun rises, imagine the rays of the sun slowly beginning to warm and relax your feet. Say to yourself, "My feet are warm, calm and quiet." Repeat this phrase a few times as you begin to release the tension from your feet and toes.

Then let the warm, life-giving sun begin to work its way up through your calves and legs. Repeat again, "My calves and legs are warm, calm and quiet." Continue to breathe deeply, and slowly, let the rising sun warm and relax your pelvis. Repeat to yourself again, "My pelvis is warm, calm and quiet." Let the tension go. There is no need to be anxious. This special place and time is just for you. You are safe here.

As the warm, tropical sun continues to rise in your mind, let the healing warmth spread through your abdominal muscles and chest. Once again, repeat silently to yourself, "My stomach and chest are warm, calm and quiet." Feel the warmth and calmness spreading from your toes, throughout your calves and legs and into your stomach and chest. Relax even further, and continue to breathe deeply.

Listen to the soothing waves and feel the warmth of the sun penetrating your shoulders and neck. We store a lot of tension in our necks, so continue to breathe and let go of the tension in your shoulders and neck. Once again, softly repeat to yourself, "My shoulders and neck are filled with the sun's warmth, and I feel calm and quiet. I feel calm and quiet." Repeat this to yourself over and over for a few moments.

Continue to breathe deeply and let the growing warmth of the healing sun relax the muscles in your face, eyes, mouth and forehead. Say to yourself, "My forehead is calm and smooth. My forehead is calm and smooth. I feel calm and quiet. I feel calm and quiet."

Continue to let the tension go, and feel the warmth and relaxation flow through the bloodstream of your body. Begin repeating, "My mind is calm and quiet. My mind is calm and quiet. My thoughts are floating in a sea of calm. My thoughts are floating in a sea of calm."

Take a few more deep breaths and softly repeat to yourself, "My body is calm and quiet. My body is calm and quiet. My thoughts are floating in a sea of calm. My mind is calm and quiet."

Continue to breathe and let your body relax. Let the anxiety just float away. You do not need it. You are safe and living in the moment of now.

If you fall asleep during this exercise, do not worry, that is good. The more you practice this technique, the more helpful it will become. As in athletic muscle training, you are teaching your muscles how to relax. After you become accustomed to this relaxing procedure, all you need to do once in awhile at work or in a stressful situation, is repeat this line in your head, "My mind and body are calm and quiet." Your body, having learned this exercise, will respond and the anxiety will disappear. Good luck.

chapter sixteen

Guilt

You feel guilty when you know you have done something *bad*. In some cases, you have not actually *done* the *bad* thing, but you have recognized in your conscious self an intention to do it. Your ego may even want to do it, but the strict superego (the governor of our actions) interjects this aggressiveness so it is internalized; it is, in fact, sent back to where it originally came from . . . your own ego. The superego (which presides over the rest of the ego) readily puts the desired action against the ego with the same aggressiveness that the ego would have liked to satisfy upon another individual. This tension between the superego and ego is called a sense of guilt, which anxiety, rage and hatred can grow out of. That guilt feels like it needs to be punished in order to subside. When you feel guilty, you deeply sense a fear of loss of love or power towards authority.

Honesty also plays an integral component in the feeling of guilt. The more dishonest you are the more guilt your superego will impose upon you. The superego will keep this pressure on your ego to stay in line and tell the truth or fear retribution for your actions. The effects of guilt on your mind and body can be devastating. From a low self-worth to the constant feeling you need to be punished.

Unexpressed feelings such as rage, hatred, anxiety, resentment and guilt are associated with strong memories and fantasies. Because these feelings are not fully expressed in awareness (consciousness), they can become repressed and are carried into day to day life in ways that interfere or inhibit effective contact with your inner self. Guilt persists until you face and deal with the unexpressed feelings. The effects of guilt often show up in some form of *blockage* to the inner self.

Resentment (anger toward something someone said or has done to you) is the most frequent and worst kind of unexpressed feeling. When you are resentful, you become *stuck* in spiritual growth. You can neither *let go* or take part in helpful communication until you express the resentment. Unexpressed resentment usually converts to guilt.

Whenever you are feeling guilty, dig deep to find out what you are resenting and express it and make your desires understood.

You must rid yourself of resentment and guilt in order to be set free in the search for your true self.

In finding yourself *stuck* you are unable to fully support yourself and thus seek support from family, friends and co-workers. Self-esteem derived from others is not a genuine source of growth for the self, and thus replaces the self-esteem that grows from within. By completely experiencing unexpressed emotions, no matter how much you would rather avoid them, you are able to get in contact with your inner, blocked frustrations. You must then act upon them, *let them go* or accept whatever it is you feel guilty of, rather than wishing situations were different. All three are easier said then done. If you can fully accept all aspects of yourself, good or bad, without judging these dimensions, you can begin to think deeply, feel, act differently, and continue on your spiritual journey. But pin-pointing the resentment and guilt is essential for this to occur. As I have said before, *letting go* of negative emotions frees up more space inside you to feel the positive emotions of love, peace and joy.

One purpose of a spiritual journey is to become whole, and we must realize in order to do so, we must *accept* the qualities we possess. Whether they be good or bad. And if we can identify those bad qualities, we can begin to work on making them better.

I would like to backtrack, for just a moment, to the purpose of a spiritual journey which is to become whole. In the movie, *Jerry Maguire* Tom Cruise's character says to his distraught wife, "You complete me." That is both a moving and powerful line in the movie and a revelation in life. To be complete, to be *whole* you *must* face the unpleasant qualities we all possess and repress. Some of my lesser qualities, as I have mentioned before, are dishonesty, little patience and a lack of full respect for others. By facing and challenging our *darker* self we can then become whole. And that revelation will lead us to accept we are not perfect.

chapter seventeen

Perfection, Control, and Anger

I highly dislike the words in the title of this chapter and what they represent. You can not be on a true spiritual journey if you suffer the consequences of one of these conditions.

I cringe when I hear someone say, *"I am a perfectionist."*

First of all, that is a lie. No matter how much we try, it is impossible to be perfect. We are not meant to be. We learn and grow from our mistakes and struggles with daily life. Every time you try and open the golden door to perfection you will run "smack dab" into a solid brick wall. Perfectionists are never happy, confident people. They can't be because it is impossible for them to be completely satisfied with any aspect of their life. Even in positive events, the perfectionist will find a negative side.

Since perfectionism can't be achieved, happiness and an inner peace with one's self can not also be attained. To try to be perfect is lying to yourself, and ultimately others, to cover up your faults.

My Personal Journal
September 22, 1996

"I decided to take a walk on the beach tonight. I found that as I relaxed, my conscious mind was already very calm, and it wasn't hard at all to pass through the barrier between the conscious and unconscious mind. I continued to fall slowly until I reached the beach. I landed in the sand close to a patchy growth of sea grass. The sight of the moon was tremendous. It had just risen high enough so the ocean could not touch it, and the reflection of the moon widened as it reached the beach . . . it is a spectacular sight. I sat there for a moment taking in the breathless scenery, and the mild, but salty, air. The pier wasn't far away, and the hanging lights upon it cast circular shadows on the weatherbeaten wood. I made my way out to God's waiting boat, and said 'I feel bad that I haven't been in touch with myself the last couple of days.'

He said, 'No one is perfect, even though you think you are, Chris. The more you try and be perfect, the less honest you will be.'

'What do you mean?' I said.

'Deep in your heart you know, Chris . . . you need not make up stories or embellish accounts of situations to your wife or parents to make them love you more. I know it can be tough with your mother, and you think accomplishments will make her love you, but that is not true. It may be hard to believe, but she loves you for just being you.'

Suddenly I felt a small weight had been taken off my shoulders, and I understood I don't need to be perfect or lie to make it appear that I am perfect or better than I am. It's okay to just be me.

Thank you, Lord. Fill me with love, and help me to keep discovering my inner self. Break down my walls, and help me to reveal my inner self."

Control and perfectionism go hand in hand. Perfectionists need to control every aspect of their careers and personal lives. This need for complete control is an overpowering urge. It is an issue of safety. Control gives the perfectionist a false sense of security, but it is ironically a shallow "mask" covering a deep feeling of insecurity.

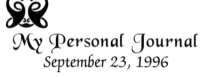

My Personal Journal
September 23, 1996

"I usually write at night. I'm not sure exactly why, maybe it's a way to empty my mind before falling asleep.

Today, though, I'm writing in the afternoon because the Lord's grace has just touched me.

I was sitting in our screened-in porch, and I was having this feeling I have had before. This very strong feeling that I'm on the edge of something. Something BIG . . . something HUGE! Something that makes me a bit anxious, but not a lot.

Then it suddenly dawned on me . . . I am living totally in the future. There is a lot that could be happening in the next few weeks. Someone could be leaving, and I could finally get what I have wanted for a year and a half.

But see I have absolutely no control over it . . . I'm going to write it again—I have **no control** over it, and that is why I feel like I am on the edge. Actually I know that is why I am, because God gave me every sign (signal) I needed to confirm my thoughts.

I was just sitting here and I said out loud, 'It's control, and I realize I have no control. Lord, I pass the control to you.' Just as I spoke those words, there was a rumble of thunder, my dog Hannah sighed, and a gorgeous butterfly flew by. It may sound crazy, but I believe God was answering me. **Let my need for control go!!** I can't control what is going to happen at work and what my company is going to do in the future. I can only do my best at my job and pray for things to work out. I believe the less I try and control, the less anxious I will feel. Thank you, Lord for this revelation. My life is in your hands, and as soon as I wrote that, the sun came out. And that golden sun strengthened my belief in 'letting go.'"

The answer to both perfectionism and control is you must "let go." As in prayer, you must surrender your life to God's will, whatever it may be. Just let it go, especially if it's in the future. (If it is in the present, and you are having trouble controlling your life, that is a different matter. We will discuss that later in the book.)

If you find "letting go" hard to do, and this may be so for perfectionists because they wear narrow "tunnel vision" glasses, just take a step back and look at your relationships and see where you can let go. Even if you have to ask your spouse or family member upfront, "Is there anything that I control that I can hand over to you.? Is there something that I control that you dislike?" The answers may shock you. Even if you don't consider yourself a "control freak," ask the questions anyway. By reaching out you are learning, living and loving.

"Letting go" is much easier than it sounds. I had a hard time giving my wife an ATM card. I was and still am very controlling when it comes to our finances, but I finally had to let go and trust my wife to be careful and keep track of what she spends. She spends a lot, but at least she gives (sometimes sneaks) me the receipts so I can keep the checkbook balanced. But that is a minor area of control. In most households one person is responsible for the financial affairs. My wife doesn't even want to see the checkbook, but in a friend's house it is just the opposite. His wife is the one who handles the finances. In both situations the one that doesn't have control could be careless about the balance in the checkbook. It's just one less thing to worry about. They have let go of that affair.

Earlier I touched upon the word *trust*. A controlling person lacks the ability to trust. Even in some stable, long-term relationships trust is hard to show and give. To trust is to "let go" and make yourself vulnerable, and many people are scared of getting hurt. And if they do, they may never trust completely again.

The sad part of a controlling relationship is the extreme conflict it can cause. I have one close friend whose wife is an extremely controlling perfectionist. She uses passive/aggressive behavior and guilt to keep her husband *under her thumb* and from doing most of the things he loves. Her controlling attitude is destructive to their marriage. Her lack of trust is obvious, and it reflects back onto insecurities of her own. To *let go* is to love. We have all heard the saying, "If you truly love someone, set them free, and if it's meant to be, they will come back to you."

Anger

Anger is an emotional roadblock on the path to spiritual growth.

Anger in me begins with the lighting of a fire under a water-filled pot. Slowly the water begins to heat up and bubble until it finally starts to boil and produce a hot steam. I find it hard to put out the fire, and the anger burns everything else around it. It burns away all the good emotions until it is the only one left. With that anger can come obsession. I begin to obsess about the cause of the powerful emotion. Usually, the cause is another person. In the heat of anger, I must concentrate extremely hard and use self-discipline before deciding how to react. If you react too quickly, you may damage the situation beyond future repair. If you don't react at all, you can risk the loss of self-esteem and feel "walked on." And then again you might just want to let the anger go because it is just not worth the effort. It depends upon you and the situation, but you must find a way to deal with anger. Because holding it in is just asking for trouble. The anger will eat away at you until it is released or it does its damage. This is just another example of how just "letting go" could be extremely beneficial.

You must learn to quickly deal with anger or risk the painful effects it will have on your spiritual journey. Anger and spirit are two words that have no similarities except for their intensity. One is completely destructive while the other is self-enlarging.

Feeling the extent of our anger is a necessary step on the path to spiritual growth. It is a common occurrence to turn the anger inward on ourselves that we do not feel safe expressing toward another person. Being angry at ourselves isolates us and undermines our ability to make meaningful connections or to reach out toward others.

The anger may become mixed up with guilt. Having the feeling *it must be my fault* can make you turn the anger inward on yourself as a way of punishing yourself. If we feel responsible, which usually occurs at this juncture, we will create a *vicious circle*. The more we feel taken advantage of, the more at fault we feel and the more we turn anger inward. This increasing anger can lead to depression, or we might even *act out* abusively toward others in an attempt to get rid of the overpowering emotion. It is for this reason we must break the *vicious circle,* feel the anger and the pain, and address it rather than suppress it. This will empower us to fight back, to stop feeling like we are the problem.

When repressed anger and pain are brought to the consciousness and felt rather than *pushed back under the rug,* it is far less likely they will be acted out unconsciously. When we are willing to take responsibility for the pain and anger we carry, our spiritual journey will continue and flourish.

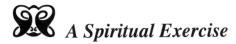 *A Spiritual Exercise*

Falling Out of My Own Garden of Eden into My Own Capital or First Sin

Committing our *own* capital sin is necessary sin, a *peccatum necessarium*, as St. Augustine said of it. We can not not do it. Not to commit it would imprison us in a purely animal consciousness that is without self-awareness and freedom of choice. Because we are created to become like unto God, in his own image and likeness, it is therefore our destiny to become *divine* with a small *d*.

In some experience of our very early childhood each of us underwent this event for which we are vaguely responsible, but not personally responsible, a deed we committed with vaguely conscious intent, at best, followed by a spontaneous sense of guilt.

If you are not already aware of your own *capital* or *first* sin, I suggest you go back in your memories to the earliest memory you have. For some, it may not be possible to go back beyond, say, age ten; for others, it may be possible to go back as far as age two, or even earlier. In either case, the exercise I am about to suggest usually does work.

Begin by placing yourself in a position comfortable for you when you are praying or meditating. Take slowly eight deep breaths, breathing in . . . , breathing out . . . Then become aware of your center (the area below the navel and above the groin).

Now begin to go back in your memory, first to the first grade of grammar school, remembering some significant experience during the first week or so of school. Then try to remember the circumstances, the place, the persons present, the most significant persons involved. Try to remember as vividly as possible the detail of what took place. Most importantly, what were you feeling? Did the feelings change? What did the person present say to you? What did you say in reply?

If possible, try to go back to the years between ages two and six and do the same procedure again.

What do you, now as an adult, understand about that experience that as a child you did not understand? You came away from the event with a flawed sense toward life in which you somehow alienated your*self* from the wholeness of reality. Most likely it was some quite simple event, perhaps the birth of an infant brother or sister:

now you are no longer Number One! Whatever it was, it became for you an unconceptualized, unarticulated norm: the basis or foundation on which you developed your way of behaving in life.

The next few pages depict nine different basic personality types and can be an aid to you in determining the *capital* sin of your basic personality.

Helps Along the Road to Self-Knowledge

Listed below in the form of a prayer are the basic personality types (adapted from the Ennegram), all of which are found within each and every one of us. But only one of these predominates. This one personality type is elicited, brought to consciousness, early in life between ages two and six by some human experience. From then on it is permanently and uniquely ours. The other types also come eventually to consciousness but will never identify us. Which of these do you most resemble? Read through all nine before reaching a conclusion. There is a tendency in all of us to deny and to resist being labelled. *No one of the nine types is better or more valid than any other. All are essential to the human condition.* The nine types divide into three groups of three: action-centered (2, 3, 4); perception-centered (5, 6, 7); and emotion-centered (8, 9, 1).

Action-Centered Personalities: (Anxiety-based)

2. Lord, I'm the nurturing type of person. I like to feel that others need me. I think you know that I am a helper. There are so many people out there who need my help. I just can't stand being all alone with nobody to take care of. I get all fidgety and restless. Why, Lord, I just don't understand how anyone could just go off and abandon his children. You'll never catch me doing anything like that, Lord, certainly not to my own children. I know they depend on their mom or dad, and couldn't possibly function without me. Much as I love them, it really hurts at times when they don't seem to appreciate all the good things I do for them. When that happens, I let them know about my dissatisfaction. Where would they be without me? And that goes for their mom or dad too. I really appreciate how devoted my spouse is to me, how much he or she completely depends on me. I remember one day, however, my

spouse telling me he or she would like now and then to go off with a couple of friends for a few days vacation. Well I put a stop to that kind of thinking. There isn't anything he or she can get from others that he or she can't get from me—all he or she needs to do is ask for it, and he or she knows that.
(Capital or First Sin Is Pride.)

3. Lord, if you know there is a job to be done, you, and anyone else, can depend on me. I am your man or woman to get the show on the road, to get the job done. Because I am such an outgoing man or woman, people always tell me I would make a great salesperson. Organization and efficiency are my middle names. And as for competency, there's not much of anything I can not do, if I put my mind to it. Yes, sir, success is the name of the game and that means to be willing to compromise.

    When it comes to competition, you know, Lord, I am always out there at the head of the pack. So, I think you can see, Lord, there is no room for failure in my approach to life. I find the more successful I am, the more people really begin to take notice of me, and I really like that. Always project a successful image. Deception is a finely honed craft among image-makers. . . . My wife or husband says I am a workaholic, that I can't relax, can't just let go and be with my own feelings. If I'm not busy at my job, I have that awful, queasy feeling of not knowing who I am.
(Capital or First Sin Is Lying.)

4. Lord, you know it is not a black-and-white world for me, that life is so richly and colorfully varied. I find it impossible to understand people who stick to a strict schedule, who pride themselves, for instance, on routinely knowing exactly what they will wear and what they will eat every day of the week. I easily become bored with the routine and the ordinary. The world is brimming over with almost unlimited potential for change, for the pursuit of new ideas and structures. Life for me is full of beauty and yet it is so often tragic. I often come away with the impression that people don't really understand me. Do they really know what it means to suffer, to be rejected? I suffer often from depression and loneliness, from a sense of not belonging . . . Why is it, Lord, that I am hardly ever sat-

isfied with whatever I have accomplished? Why is it I always end up saying, "Is that all?" There has to be more than this. I hope it is true that life begins at forty because it seems I have hardly gotten off the pad ... It is when I get completely absorbed in my piano playing or my art work that the hours fly by without me even noticing. People tell me I have a flair for the artistic and the dramatic, that I'm also given to exaggeration and diminishment.
(Capital or First Sin Is Envy.)

Perception-Centered Personalities: (Fear-based)

5. Lord, I am something of a loner. By that I mean I don't care much for meetings. But if I have to attend them, I am very observant and perceptive, taking in everything that is being said. I can sum up and integrate the various suggestions and ideas that others have presented during the entire discussion. But unless asked, I probably will not take the initiative. If people ask me about my feelings, I tend to draw a blank. I feel embarrassed because I guess I really don't pay much attention to my feelings and I would not be inclined to share them with others. I tend to solve my problems by thinking. I'm not given to spontaneous reactions or responses. I need time to sort things out before venturing a public response. It seems I can never get enough information on any given topic. I'm forever buying books, some of which I never get around to reading. I am always craving for more, both intellectually and materially. And I don't like letting go of what I have acquired.
(Capital or First Sin Is Greed.)

6. Lord, I am afraid I don't have much self-confidence, much inner authority. I need to feel certain about things, especially the essential things of life, both physically and mentally. And because of this craving I can easily get caught up in doubt and scrupulosity. So I am a cautious person. But I am also a very loyal person and obedient. Once I have thought the matter through, I can open up new paths, forge new frontiers. I could probably even give my life for a truly worthy cause.

It's the either/or world, the world of black and white, of law and order, that makes for safety, something I can never get

enough of. But fear can eat away at my faith because of my craving for certainty and safety. And the loyalty I boast of can often be a cover-up for my many unmanageable fears. Yet in moments of crisis I can jettison all of my fears and do heroic deeds/ Lord, teach me not to fear you out of slavery to the fear of death, but to revere and respect you out of a sense of awe and wonder.
(Capital or First Sin Is Cowardly Fear.)

7. Lord, I just want to thank you for all the wonderful things you have given me throughout my life. I guess it is true that there were some hard times, but I always try not to dwell on such hard times. I always see the bright and pleasurable side of life. I'm a firm believer in putting on a happy face, whistling a happy tune. Life has always been such a joy for me, so I try to avoid the crepe-hangers of this world. I find that a funny story or a good joke is a cure for most any problem. The more fun, the better, I always say, Lord. I thank you for the great sense of humor you gave me. Some of my friends often tell me they think I run away from life by forever seeing only the funny or pleasant side of life. They say I spend too much time day-dreaming and making plans for the future. But as I see it, life is so full of good things that I am afraid I won't have enough time to enjoy them all, and to the fullest. Thanks again, Lord, for a great life.
(Capital or First Sin Is Gluttony.)

Emotion-Centered Personalities: (Anger-based)

8. Lord, I have a passion for stimulation in most areas of experience and a special passion for truth and justice, ready to do all in my power to uphold them. I come at life from a position of strength. I feel there isn't much of anything I can not do, if I put my mind to it. I'm true to my word, and responsible. I'll challenge anyone I suspect of dishonesty and shame. I don't kowtow to anyone or anything, especially pain. I challenge! Whoever knows me knows I am the boss. I never admit to weakness, but feel it is my job to protect the weak and defenseless and to defend the oppressed.

When it comes to expressing anger, that is my forte to get

the other guy to bow to my superiority. Anyone who challenges me is looking at defeat. It's my job to challenge. If there is anything I can not stand, it's the coward and the *softy*. I pride myself in being in the know, and woe to the idiot who tries to outfox me.

(Capital or First Sin Is Lust.)

9. Lord, my motto is: Don't rock the boat! People sometimes call me lazy, but that is not really the case; it's more like psychological and spiritual inertia. It has more to do with a lack of energy for exploring my inner world. I am content with things as they are. I resist change. In many ways I am a creature of habit. As I always say, nothing is so urgent that it can't wait until tomorrow.

I guess I just don't see myself as being all that important to get all fired up about any one given issue. So I tend to be very laid back when it comes to decision-making, and sometimes I can get so stuck on an issue that people tell me: "Well either _____ or get off the pot!" But on the other hand, once I decide, wild horses could not divert me from my determined path.

People tell me I am good at seeing both sides of most any issue. And that is true because I am not wedded to either side. I am a great one for conserving energy. *Conservative* is certainly a label that can be pinned on me. But keep in mind what I said about decision-making . . . If I hanker after anything, it is creature comforts, like watching football and basketball games and just plain survival.

(Capital or First Sin Is Sloth.)

1. Lord, the proper description of me is that I am a hard worker with a strong penchant for correctness. If there is anything I can't stand, it is sloppy thinking or the haphazard and imprecise approach to life. My parents always taught me to do what is right, to be honest and always respectful of legitimate authority. I admit that I can be a stickler for detail, finding fault with things most people would not notice or consider noticing. *Perfectionist* is probably the correct label for a person like me.

Lord, when I look at all the injustice in the world, I know that it isn't right. The world ought not to be like that and I feel it is my job to work unceasingly and, if necessary, to fight for a truly just world. I know that one day I will have to render an account of myself; so with that always in mind, I strive to always be the most responsible person.
(Capital or First Sin Is Anger.)

Remember, only one of these predominates. This one personality type is elicited, brought to consciousness, early in life between ages two and six by some human experience. The other types eventually come to consciousness, but *will never fully identify us as one in particular.* **Which of these do you most resemble? Be honest with yourself, and then begin to slowly work on the upsetting parts.**

chapter eighteen

Fear

Fear is a projection from the past. You fear the future will bring you negative emotions and results. As long as these projections continue, you will keep coming up with fearful situations to accommodate what has already happened. You can learn from the past, but do not fear it. The events you fear in the future are just reflections in the mirror of the past.

Love of yourself grows when you refuse to follow the feeling of fear. Trust and have faith that life is on your side, seek the desires in your heart and soul, and watch with joy as your inner self carries them out. Believe in **yourself** strongly, unconditionally, and respect the gentleness and passion of your love for others. Always think and feel positive, try carrying out your needs and desires without seeking anyone else's approval.

🐏 My Personal Journal
July 12, 1996

"I have taken a few days off with my wife and have gone to St. Louis with her to see her parents.

Yesterday, I arrived and had a tranquil day and night. Just what I needed. Kris (my wife) had driven out two days earlier. I had stayed behind to watch over inspections on the new house. Anyway, I arrived yesterday and was really able to 'let go' a little of the stuff going on in Kansas City. I sat with my father-in-law, Ted, and smoked a few cigars, met one of Kris's friends, and was waited on hand and foot by Mary. She is a wonderful and sweet mother-in-law. I got real lucky, or maybe I should say it was the grace of God that I received such great and caring in-laws.

Ted (with deep love and respect I now call him Dad) and I seem to be getting much closer. He is a remarkable man. Still searching for the truth, providing for his family, but most importantly he continues his spiritual journey at the age of sixty-eight. I have learned from him what hard work and dedication can bring you. But on the flipside, it is no secret he works far too much. He fears if he stops working he will stop growing. Ted should take more time and live in the present. Something I am continually trying to do, but find so difficult."

The answer to fear is quite simple. If you are living in the present, the moment of now, you are already safe, and if you feel safe fear will not overwhelm you.

The preeminent fear, though, for all of us is the fear of death. Modern day psychology speaks to us that death is the most extreme example of loss. So any loss—being fired from your job, losing your house or apartment, losing money in a business deal gone wrong—creates a deep unconscious horror that parallels the ultimate fear of death. We have learned that clinging to life is the only way to face death. That is wrong. Our conception and fear of death comes from our projections into what death possibly is. We are scared of the *nothingness* of death . . . that we will just cease to exist. This is a response rooted in fear, and only when we stop clinging to life can we hope to catch a glimpse of the reality that lies underneath our created illusion of death. Presumably finding out what occurs after death. The scriptures call this "dying unto death." In other words, dying to the *known* which brings us knowledge about death.

I do not pretend to have all the answers. I have learned, though, that faith and love is much stronger than the fear of death. Living in the moment of now is much stronger than the fear of death. Look at death as a *transition,* not an end to existence. Christ Himself feared death, but Our Heavenly Father was waiting, in a sea of love, on the other side.

Fear is a massive roadblock along our spiritual journey. We **must** *let go* of bad experiences we had in the past, and not let them influence our thoughts of the future. Because there could be no future. You **must** "live one day at a time."

chapter nineteen

One More Time
Letting Go

🦋 *An Emotional Exercise*

$\mathcal{T}$his uncovering exercise is designed to free you of all negative emotions and fears of the past and future. By releasing or *letting go* of anger, resentment, guilt, fear, frustration and failure you are freeing up more space in your heart and spirit to let love, peace and joy fill in those previously occupied spaces. Thus, you will begin to realize more of your own self-love, and love of others that ultimately go hand in hand. Your ego does not want this to occur. It wants to hold on to these destructive emotions so your rough, protecting outer shell can be strong and it will appear that you can't be hurt. This is nothing but further from the truth.

First, find a place where you will not be disturbed and where you can relax, quietly concentrate and feel deep into the layers that cover your heart.

Close your eyes and take a few deep breaths, in through your nose and out through your mouth. As you breathe, let your attention rest on your feeling heart. This place is right in the middle of your chest.

Continue taking deep breaths, and with every one you take in, let it fill that space. After several minutes, when you begin to fully relax, ask gently for your heart to express itself. You will be amazed at the memories and emotions that begin to rise to the surface. These memories could include old arguments, memories of past, hurtful situations or recent negative emotions. Whatever it is, let it just happen. Do not force it to occur. As each memory or emotion arises to your consciousness, examine it, and then "let it go." Just say to yourself, "I let it go. It serves no further purpose." The experience will be a cleansing one, allowing your heart to release pent-up and stuck emotions.

For example, a strong anger over a frustrating situation could come to your conscious attention. Why hold on to that anger? It is useless, and taking up much needed space in your heart where more positive emotions could replace that anger.

The hard part is *letting go,* but if you can accomplish this, you will experience an inner peace and love that will change your perception of the here and now. Consider what it would be like to be rid of anger and hatred and have a heart and soul filled with simple peace and love. By *letting go* you are opening your heart and soul for new and stimulating love and a passion for life in its purest form.

A Few More Thoughts . . .

chapter twenty

The Story of Fuzzy and Stripe

(Author's Note: I have been told by a close friend this short story is similar to one that appears in a children's book. I have not read or heard of that book. I apologize for any similarities. None were ever intended.)

The early days of summer were warm, and the freshness of new life was alive in the air. Deep in the backyard of an old but beautiful house, intertwined in an iron fence that long ago had lost its luster, was a lush green vine that every spring and summer grew tall and strong up towards the life-giving sun. This summer was no exception. As a matter of fact, the vine was taller than ever before.

Living near the bottom of the vine were two caterpillars who had become close friends. Each one had deep aspirations of reaching the top of the vine to see the top of the world and what the ultimate view would look like.

The two caterpillars, one named Fuzzy and the other called Stripe, had long discussions as the sun set on what the journey to the top would hold. Stripe believed all the answers to their existence would come from reaching the top. Fuzzy agreed outwardly, but deep inside he questioned whether or not it would be that easy to find all the answers.

After days of planning the two furry friends decided it was time to make their long-anticipated journey. The night before Stripe could hardly sleep. When he did doze off he had brillant dreams of reaching the top and meeting God. And God would answer all his questions such as, "Why did you create us? And what is the meaning for our existence?" Fuzzy, however, slept soundly. He dreamt of change and finding an inner peace he longed for. When he awoke he was confused by his dreams of change but was somehow happy even so.

They started out early on a bright and warm day. The vine was still slightly damp with the morning's dew. In the distance they could hear the soft roar of a lawnmower. They had seen one every few days in their backyard so they knew the sound well. As they climbed the vine their excitement grew and, as they looked back towards the safety of the ground below, their anxiety also grew.

By noon they had crept and crawled to near the midpoint of the vine. The sun was strong, and the day was growing hot. Fuzzy was beginning to have second thoughts about the rest of their journey. From this view the world did not look much different. Fuzzy could just see the old house at a different angle. He thought it needed a fresh coat of paint. On the other hand, Stripe was ecstatic, and dead set on making it to the top. If he made the peak, he still believed all his questions would be answered. He would rule, and see everything the world had to offer. He would be powerful and have due respect.

As they rested for a moment, Fuzzy decided he had achieved his desire. He told Stripe he would wait here for him to return. Stripe was bewildered. "Don't you want to reach the top and see all there is to this world?" Fuzzy replied, "I have seen enough, and I am content staying here." Stripe was dumbfounded, "All right, but see if I tell you the answers we seek." Fuzzy said nothing. Somewhere, deep inside his soul, told him to just stay and think deeply.

Stripe, with the energy of anger burning inside, began to climb feverishly toward the top. His passion for power and reaching the *top* consumed him. Hours passed and Stripe was exhausted but he pressed on.

As Stripe continued his climb, Fuzzy had time to contemplate life. He had this deep desire to look inward; inward to his true emerging self. Suddenly, he let go of his fears, and let God take control. Fuzzy began to spin a cocoon. It was a scary process, enclosing himself in total seclusion. Fuzzy thought, "Will I ever be set free?"

Stripe was close . . . so close he could feel it. He was mere inches away, and he was dead tired. His vision was slightly blurred, but he wanted so badly to reach the top. "The top. The top," he repeated over and over.

In the darkness of Fuzzy's cocoon he began to feel changes. He wondered if he had done the right thing. He had so much time to think about the future, about the past, about God. Then, suddenly, Fuzzy was calm. He was going to just enjoy the present; the moment of now. A few moments later, an amazing thing occurred. He wanted to burst out and enjoy the precious present with his friend Stripe.

Stripe had reached the top! He was exhausted and disappointed. The view was different, but it was lonely here at the top. He looked for God, but just saw a house on the other side of the fence. He wondered what his friend Fuzzy was doing. He felt sorry for being angry at Fuzzy.

Suddenly, an angelic butterfly landed next to Stripe. For a moment he was frightened. Then a familiar voice said, "Stripe, it is me Fuzzy. Look, I can fly everywhere!"

Stripe could hardly believe his eyes. Fuzzy was a colorful, exquisite butterfly. Fuzzy said, "Look inward, my close friend . . . look deep inside . . . look for God inside you, and you will be set free. Then we can fly together."

chapter twenty-one

The Twelve Priorities of Life

Keep this list in mind as you go about your daily spiritual life. Having a list of priorities is self-enlarging and a continual learning experience.

1. God or a higher power

2. Family

3. Love . . . True, deep, passionate and understanding love

4. Keep Some of Life Simple
      Find a special place inside yourself where you can *let go* and *forgive*

5. Happiness, joy and true friendship

6. Sharing (Risking vulnerability)

7. Reaching out and helping others discover all of the above

8. Nature . . . Enjoying that great gift God has given you
      The beauty and serenity of nature

9. A continuing spiritual journey with God or a higher power

10. Taking time to think on a deep level

11. There is not much time to truly love . . . Don't hold love
    back
        Open your heart and true self to others

12. Live in the moment of now . . . Not the future or the past

All these priorities can be incorporated in your life. It is not a list of
do one at a time or do one and not the others. Actually, it is impossible to do just one because they ultimately lead to the others.

God Bless You!
Chris Snyder, May 1997

About the Author

Chris Snyder is currently a weather anchor for KCTV 5 in Kansas City. He is also pursuing his doctorate in clinical psychology. Chris has been married for eight years to his wife Kris. They have a two-year-old son named Taylor. For questions, comments or suggestions he can be reached at:

Chris Snyder
5427 Johnson Drive Suite 178
Mission, Kansas 66205

All correspondence will be answered by author.

Notes

Notes

Notes